A Most Inconvenient Murder

"Me," I said. "I'm in Swartz's apartment. We found him on the floor, as dead as the *Herald-Trib.* Skull dented, lots of blood. Look like he's been here several hours. Instructions?"

Wolfe took one of his bushel-sized breaths, then cleared his throat. "Have you talked to the police?" His tone was grim.

"Not yet. I thought you might have some sage thoughts at this point."

"*Pfui.* It's too late for sagacity, assuming you would recognize it if it were proffered to you. You must of course summon them."

"Believe it or not, that was next on my list of chores. You realize it will mean long hours of questioning and missed meals for yours truly."

"I do," Wolfe said. I swear he almost sounded sympathetic.

• *A NERO WOLFE MYSTERY* •

FADE TO BLACK

Robert Goldsborough

BANTAM BOOKS

NEW YORK • TORONTO • LONDON • SYDNEY • AUCKLAND

The author wishes to thank the estate of the
late Rex Stout for their cooperation and support.

*This edition contains the complete text
of the original hardcover edition.*
NOT ONE WORD HAS BEEN OMITTED.

FADE TO BLACK

*A Bantam Crime Line Book
Bantam hardcover edition / November 1990
Bantam rack edition / September 1991*

CRIME LINE *and the portrayal of a boxed "cl" are trademarks of
Bantam Books, a division of Bantam Doubleday Dell Publishing Group, Inc.*

Library of Congress Catalog Card Number: 90-511

ISBN 0-553-29264-1

Published simultaneously in the United States and Canada

Bantam Books are published by Bantam Books, a division of Bantam Doubleday Dell Publishing Group, Inc. Its trademark, consisting of the words "Bantam Books" and the portrayal of a rooster, is Registered in U.S. Patent and Trademark Office and in other countries. Marca Registrada. Bantam Books, 666 Fifth Avenue, New York, New York 10103.

PRINTED IN THE UNITED STATES OF AMERICA

OPM 0 9 8 7 6 5 4 3 2 1

To Steve Rubin
for getting me started

and

To Kate Miciak
for keeping me on track

ONE

The whole business started at Lily Rowan's Super Bowl party. If that sounds cryptic—good; I read someplace once that the best way to hook a reader at the start of a story is with something cryptic, so there you are.

Anyway, around Thanksgiving Lily got the idea she should toss a big Super Bowl bash in her penthouse palace on East Sixty-third just off Park Avenue. For years, Lily and I have been what some might choose to call "special friends," and in all that time, I never detected in her even the merest flicker of interest in pro football. Baseball, basketball, and hockey are different stories—I can always coax her to Shea or the Garden for a game.

"Oh, you know me," she said when I expressed surprise about the proposed festivities, "I don't care a fig for the game, for heaven's sake. It's just such a wonderful excuse to get people together in the middle of the winter—at least those who haven't gone off to Gstaad or St. Moritz or the Caribbean." That might sound like place-dropping, but given many of the people Lily knows, it's simply accurate reporting. As it turned out, I wasn't all that excited about the Super Bowl myself. Both teams were from burgs more than a thousand miles from Manhattan, and the strongest offensive weapon each had was a sawed-off field-goal kicker with an unpronounceable Middle-European name.

But never mind the football, the party on that January Sunday exceeded even Lily's usual lavish standards. It drew a shade over a hundred of her nearest and dearest friends, at least those who had passed up Switzerland or the islands. A tuxedoed, five-piece band usually booked into the Churchill Hotel's Velvet Lounge made sweet sounds in the sun room. Red-jacketed mixologists poured drinks at bars in the living room, game room, and den, and waitresses moved through the crowd every thirteen seconds with trays of canapés, shrimp, fresh vegetables, quiche, and assorted other goodies. The game itself was on six screens in various rooms, although well over half of the guests were more interested in mingling than in rooting for guys in red-and-gold or brown-and-white uniforms. The hostess, looking lovely in a light gray number and gold shoes, moved smoothly from cluster to cluster, pausing to talk to everyone—even me, her escort. "See, darling," she whispered, giving me an impish look, "nobody cares about that damnable game. They're here to eat, drink, dance, and Lord knows, maybe even gossip."

"Who can quarrel with those lofty goals?" said I, brushing her dusty blond hair with a hand and enjoying the scent of Uninhibited. She drifted off toward another group and I found myself talking to a couple named Pembroke that Lily and I had sat with at a benefit dinner a couple of years back. They hadn't become any more interesting in the interim, so I excused myself to get a drink at the nearest bar, where I ran into a glum-faced, sandy-haired guy who bore a more than middling resemblance to Robert Redford.

He introduced himself as Rod Mills. "And you're Archie Goodwin, the detective—right?" he asked, sticking out a firm paw. I pled guilty, and while we both stirred our Scotches, I inquired as to what he did for a living, to be polite.

He shrugged deprecatingly. "Advertising."

"Would I know your work?" I asked, still in the polite mode.

"You might," he answered, scratching the back of his neck. "Our biggest account—we're Mills/Lake/Ryman—is Cherr-o-key. You know, the soft drink."

"Sure. Say, didn't I read something in the *Times* or the *Gazette* last week about a spectacular Cherr-o-key commercial that's going to be on during the Super Bowl?"

"Why do you think I'm keeping one eye on that stupid screen? Certainly not because of the game." He gestured dismally toward the nearest tube. "It's going to be shown at halftime—the network willing. I quit smoking two years ago, but God, I could use a cigarette now."

"Rod! Come on, I'm getting everybody together in the game room, where they've got the big screen!" The voice was breathless, and it belonged to a svelte creature who probably made most of the men she met breathless, too. "Hi," she bubbled to me, tossing long black hair in a practiced but pleasing manner. "I'm Dawn Tillison."

"Ah, yes, Lily has mentioned you," I said with a

slight bow. "You've worked together on a charity board, right?"

"That's right, Mr. . . ."

"Dawn, this is Archie Goodwin," Mills said. "He's—"

"Oh, now I know—he's Lily's good friend," she put in, appraising me with purple eyes. I sensed a shrewdness beneath the surface effervescence. "I recognize the name. I've heard so much about you, Mr. Goodwin—it's a real pleasure." Those see-all eyes danced when she said it, making me want to believe every word that passed her nicely formed lips. I assured her the pleasure was mutual, but that it would increase exponentially if she'd call me Archie. She solemnly promised she would, but it was clear that at the moment, all she could think about was Mills's commercial. "Come on, hurry," she said to both of us, taking a somber Mills by the hand and smiling at me. I trotted along and found myself joined by one L. Rowan, who linked her arm in mine.

"I see you've met Rod and Dawn," she said as we fell a few steps behind them. "Aren't they a good-looking couple?"

"I hadn't studied *him* terribly closely," I told her, getting a light dig in the ribs as a reward for my honesty. "Still avoiding the game?"

"I haven't watched an instant of it," Lily purred, "but I was just told that I'm sixty dollars ahead in a pool, something about points scored. I don't understand it. All I know is a group in the sun room was putting together this pool thing before the game started and I threw in ten dollars, just to be sociable. I didn't even pay any attention to the numbers I drew, but they wrote them down in squares on some sort of a chart."

"A little more of that kind of sociability on your part, and all of your millionaire guests will go home broke. Say, how do you happen to know Mills?"

"Rod? Oh, through Dawn—she's been going out with him for three or four months. He's divorced, and apparently is very successful in advertising, so she tells me, although she's hardly unbiased. She's crazy about him."

Just then Dawn Tillison hushed the crowd, or at least the thirty or so of us who had squeezed into the game room. "Here it comes," she said excitedly. "Everybody quiet now."

"I feel like I'm on a movie set about to watch Streep and Nicholson in action," I whispered to Lily, who tugged at my sleeve to shut me up. The rest of the buzzing subsided, and for several seconds, we all watched a station break that informed us in multicolored, computer-generated words and graphics and reverential tones that there was more to come on the "Super Bowl Halftime Spec-TAC-u-lar!"

"This is it," Dawn injected unnecessarily as the familiar "Breaking Free with Cherr-o-key" theme song assaulted our ears—sung, I later learned, by the hottest of the new British rock groups. The giant screen exploded with single-engine planes flying in formation, filmed at different angles from other planes or helicopters. Then, simultaneously, tiny figures dropped from each of the planes and hurtled earthward, causing gasps in the darkened room.

Next, again almost simultaneously, parachutes with the red-and-yellow Cherr-o-key logo on them burst open above each of the plummeting figures, and they floated to earth, all landing in a field while the rock group pounded home the theme. Each of the skydivers, photogenic young men and women in red-and-yellow jumpsuits emblazoned with the soft drink's logo, were shown moments after they alighted, triumphantly holding up cans of Cherr-o-key that they presumably had clutched to their contented bosoms as they floated earthward.

The instrumental volume soared. The skydivers popped the tops of their cans in unison, leaned back, and began pouring the red stuff down their throats to the heavenly lyrics ". . . breaking free with Cherr-o-key, oh yes, oh yes . . . Cherr-o-key and you and me, oh yes, oh yes . . ." The closing shot, taken from the air, showed the divers joining hands and forming a large C around one of the parachutes, neatly laid out on the ground to display the bright logo. As the screen faded to black, applause broke out spontaneously. There were cries of "Way to go, Rod!" and "Good show!" and "How many skydivers were there?"

"Sixteen," Mills shot back, passing a handkerchief over his forehead. He looked to be more nervous than the coaches of the Super Bowl teams. "I should know—I had to authorize the damned insurance for each and every one of 'em. And for sixteen pilots, too. And you should have seen the bill for renting the planes—not to mention the choppers."

Laughter followed and a half-dozen people lined up to shake hands with the perspiring adman before moving back to their respective game-watching seats or conversation groups. Dawn Tillison was last in the receiving line. She put her arms around Mills, kissing him and whispering something that caused his ears to turn red. I looked discreetly away and made for the bar.

I was stirring my refill when Mills walked up and ordered, his ears now more or less back to their normal color. "You've earned that drink," I told him. "That was some production."

"Thanks," he said, exhaling noisily. "I'm glad *that's* over. It took a lot of work by a lot of people, to say nothing of money."

"I can imagine. Were the kids on the ground drinking Cherr-o-key the same ones who'd jumped?"

Mills took a healthy swig of his Scotch, then shook his head. "That's part of what made the spot so damn expensive. Skydivers are an okay-looking bunch on the whole, but we wanted *beautiful* for the close-ups, you know? The skydivers—we got them from clubs in California, where the commercial was shot about six weeks ago—their part was over the second they hit the ground. The bunch in the closeups were actors and models—another sixteen people to pay. Not to mention the camera crews in the other planes and the choppers."

"Well, cost aside, you've got to be feeling pretty good right now," I told him.

The adman let his shoulders sag. "I'm just glad the thing has run. Oh, given what it cost to put together, it'll be on again, sometimes in shorter versions—this one was sixty seconds. But the Super Bowl slot was the big one." He set his drink carefully on the bar and gave me a thoughtful look. "You know, originally Dawn and

I were going to watch the game at my place, just the two of us. But then we got the invitation from Lily, and I remembered that you and she are, well . . ."

"Friends?"

"Right. I guess I must have read it somewhere, maybe in one of the columns, or maybe Dawn mentioned it once. Anyway, I figured you'd be at any party Lily gave, and I wanted to meet you."

"Okay, I'll bite—why?"

He frowned and rubbed his chin. Despite the apparent success of the ad, his expression remained troubled. "I know Nero Wolfe doesn't take on very many cases—I read that somewhere, too. But I was hoping to interest him, and you, of course, in a problem our agency is having . . ."

"You're right about Mr. Wolfe. On his priority scale, work is somewhere down around visiting the dentist for a root canal job. Care to tell me a little bit about it? Sometimes I can get him interested, or at least irritated enough with me to consider accepting a fee, if only to shut me up." What I didn't mention was that our bank account, although not anemic, could stand a healthy transfusion. It had been nearly three months since Wolfe had added to the treasury by noodling out which of seven officers had been embezzling from a bank in a little Connecticut burg.

Mills shot the hovering bartender a wary look, and we took our drinks and moved away to a corner out of earshot. He still looked uncomfortable—and glum—but after sampling Lily's Scotch a time or two more, he indulged himself in another deep breath and started in.

"I don't know how familiar you are with the advertising world, so if I'm being too elementary, tell me. First off, it's hellishly cutthroat, particularly when you're dealing with products—or services—that are themselves in a cutthroat market. And dammit, there's nothing much more cutthroat than soft drinks."

"As in Coke versus Pepsi? I don't watch TV all that much, but when I do, it seems like one of the two has a commercial running every fifteen minutes."

"Yeah, and also as in Cherr-o-key versus Ameri-Cherry, although their ad budgets aren't in the same league with Coke and Pepsi. However, cherry drinks are really hot right now. Personally I can't stand 'em," he said, lowering his voice and making a face, "but I'm telling you, at the moment they can't make the stuff fast enough."

"So what's the problem?"

"The problem is, AmeriCherry . . ." He sighed, as if he hated to pronounce the name. "AmeriCherry, our client's big competitor, has a mole in our shop, or so it seems."

"Mole—as in industrial espionage?"

Mills nodded, sawing his lower lip with his teeth. "Yeah, in effect. For the last two major Cherr-o-key campaigns we've planned, AmeriCherry beat us out with practically the identical execution."

"Great minds, et cetera?"

"No way. These were too damned close to be co-incidences. My partners and I are absolutely convinced that our creative is getting leaked to the agency that handles AmeriCherry."

"You talked to anybody over there about it?"

"Hell, no. Those arrogant bastards—it's Colmar and Conn—are probably twenty-five times our size, if not more. Besides, if there is a leak, which seems sure, it's got to be starting in our place, or with people we use."

"So you're suggesting that Mr. Wolfe find the leak?"

"We sure haven't had any luck trying to plug it ourselves." Mills sounded bitter.

"Well, they didn't beat you on the skydiving thing," I said.

He allowed himself a sour smile. "No, but that was pretty much a one-shot blockbuster, rather than a continuing campaign, although it cost several hundred thou, about as much as a whole campaign. And even with the blockbuster, I've been worried stiff we'd see something like it out of the competition before today. I really was, and so were my partners. They've probably been sitting in front of their TV sets at home sweating just like I have here."

"I must tell you that this isn't the kind of job Mr. Wolfe normally takes," I cautioned. "I won't completely rule it out, but for one thing, he's not a great fan of either television or advertising." I could have been less diplomatic in my phrasing, as in Wolfe loathes most of what's on the tube and virtually all the advertising he sees, both on TV and in the papers and magazines, but I saw no reason to alienate a possible client.

"But he does like money," Mills countered.

"Inarguably."

Mills leaned forward, setting his jaw. His face had taken on an unhealthy tinge. "Mr. Goodwin—Archie—for our agency, this is serious on a cosmic level. We're fairly new, and growing, but we're not exactly large yet, probably never will be, which is all right. Cherr-o-key is far and away our biggest account. The agency's income this year will be around four and a half million, piddling compared to the big guys, and Cherr-o-key will account for about two million eight, or a little better than sixty percent of the bottom line. Without them, we're hurting both in the financial and the prestige departments, to say nothing of how many people we'd have to lay off if we lost their business. We—that includes my two partners, Boyd Lake and Sara Ryman—desperately need to meet with Mr. Wolfe."

I studied Mills as he talked and decided that his problem was worth incurring the irritation of the czar who signs my checks. "Okay, I will take this up with him either tonight or tomorrow morning."

"I appreciate that," he said, nodding soberly and handing me his card. "I'm glad we were able to talk."

"Me too. After all, the alternative was watching the dullest football game since they outlawed the flying wedge."

That actually got a chuckle out of him, which was something. This was a man who didn't look like he'd been laughing much lately.

TWO

By the time I got home to the old brownstone on West Thirty-fifth Street a few minutes before midnight Sunday, the office was dark, which meant that Wolfe had retired to his bedroom on the second floor. I quickly followed suit, taking the stairs two at a time to my own room one floor above his, happy I hadn't spent more than a half-dozen minutes watching a snoozer of a Super Bowl that ended with a score of nine to six—nothing but field goals.

The next morning found me as usual in the kitchen at my small table, eating sausage and wheatcakes prepared by Fritz Brenner and reading the *Times.* Wolfe always has breakfast in his bedroom from a tray carried up by Fritz, then goes directly to the plant rooms on the roof to play with his orchids until eleven.

I skimmed the Super Bowl coverage on the sports pages, where the *Times* reporters agreed that it was the most boring of these roman-numeraled games to date. The marketing columnist had some good words for the Cherr-o-key skydiving commercial, though, calling it "easily the liveliest, most entertaining sixty seconds of the entire four-hour spectacle." He pointed out that it had been a product of the creative engine of Mills/Lake/Ryman and named the three partners. The columnist summed up his report by calling the agency "New York's hottest new small shop."

"Fritz, what does the word 'Cherr-o-key' mean to you?" I asked after pouring myself a second cup of coffee.

"Very sad, Archie, very sad," he answered, pressing his lips together. "Indians—they call them Native Americans now, of course. They had to leave their homes and go many miles west, driven by evil men. It was called the 'Trail of Tears.' "

"You always amaze me. How did you know that?"

He shrugged, turning back to the griddle, where my next cake was cooking. "I read," he said in an apologetic tone.

"You sure do," I told him. Fritz lives in the basement of the brownstone, in a cozy two-room apartment he's made into a home over the years, and it's filled with books and magazines.

"You ever heard the word 'Cherr-o-key' on television?" I persisted.

"I watch the TV very little, Archie," he said, laying another steaming wheatcake on my plate. "Mostly the news at eleven."

"What about the commercials?"

"Ah, but I never hear them—I can shut the noise off. The button, you know?" He held up a hand and cocked his thumb.

"Right. Remote control. The viewer's best friend, the advertiser's worst enemy." Fritz looked at me without reaction. It was hard to fault his taste.

After finishing breakfast, I carried a cup of coffee

to my desk in the office and began entering orchid germination records into the personal computer. Theodore Horstmann, who has been employed in the brownstone even longer than I have, oversees those ten thousand plants up on the roof that Wolfe calls his "concubines." Normally Theodore takes Sundays off, but this week he made an exception because he'd been sick for several days. And on each day that he works, he unfailingly logs germination information in precise handwriting on three-by-five cards, leaving them on my desk on the way out the door in the evening. I think he takes perverse pleasure in dropping work on me, which is fair, I suppose; I don't like him much, either.

After I finished entering the orchid data, I did the letters Wolfe had dictated Saturday, again using the computer, I printed them out and put them on his blotter. Next, I turned to the phone to call Lon Cohen of the *New York Gazette.* For those of you who are new to these narratives, Lon has no title I'm aware of at the largest evening newspaper in the United States, but he has more power than most editors on any paper, and he occupies an office two doors from the publisher on the twentieth floor. For years, Wolfe and I have traded information with Lon, which has resulted in scoops for the *Gazette* and money in the checking account for us. Also, he's one hell of a poker player, and I should know: He's been helping to lighten my wallet for years at our Thursday night games in Saul Panzer's apartment. And even Saul, the best player I've ever seen, gets burned with some frequency by Lon—take last week, when Saul held three jacks but folded on the biggest pot of the night because he was positive Lon had a flush. We'll never know for sure, but whatever

ESP I possess tells me that Lon Cohen was not holding five spades.

Anyway, Lon, who comes to dinner at the brownstone periodically, is both friend and business associate, a balancing act that has been maintained over the years—not without occasional strain. This might be one of those occasions, I mused, as I finished punching out his number. On the second ring, I got the usual harried "*Gazette*—Cohen."

"Goodwin," I shot back.

"What do you want?"

"Can't a fellow make a social call once in a while?" I answered, trying to sound hurt.

"Sure, but you're not the social call type," Lon retorted.

"Well . . . I *do* have one small question."

"Of course you do. Well, out with it, then. We've got deadlines here, y'know."

"So I've heard. What do you know about the advertising agency Mills/Lake/Ryman?"

"Not a lot. It's a small shop, fairly new, but they've got a good creative reputation, according to our ad columnist. He thinks they're comers. I suppose you know they did that splashy parachute number for the cherry drink on the Super Bowl yesterday."

"Yeah. Heard any dirt on the partners or anybody else in the agency?"

"Nope, nothing. What gives—Wolfe thinking of starting to advertise his services on TV?"

"That'll be the day," I laughed. "No, although it might help us get some business. Will you check with your ad guy to see if there's ever been anything amiss about the agency?"

"Okay, but it's unlikely. Archie, is there something I should know?"

"No, and there probably won't be. Just doing some checking."

"Well, keep your old pal posted."

"I will. So long, old pal," I said, hanging up just as I heard the whine of the elevator: His eminence was descending from his sojourn with the aforesaid orchids.

"Good morning, Archie. Did you sleep well?" Wolfe detoured around his desk and eased into the only chair expressly constructed to bear the burden of his seventh of a ton.

I said I had indeed slept well, briefly mentioned Lily's party, then asked, as I had Fritz, what 'Cherr-o-key' meant to him.

My answer was a glower. "What is behind this?" he grunted. "You never pose queries capriciously."

I grinned. "Maybe it was capricious, maybe not. You can find out by answering it—if you can."

Wolfe considered me without enthusiasm. "The Cherokees are a tribe of North American aboriginals, or, to use the contemporary term, Native Americans. Arguably the most progressive and well-organized tribe in what is now the United States, they centered in the southern Appalachians, principally North Carolina. But with the coming of Europeans, many were forcibly uprooted and driven west, to the Oklahoma Indian Territory. That barbaric thousand-mile march became known as the 'Trail of Tears.' "

"That's just about what Fritz said when I asked him the same question."

"And why not? Fritz is no lackwit. The Cherokees' history is generally known."

"Not to me, but never mind. Speaking of Cherokees, I was reviewing our finances just before you came down."

"That's a non sequitur."

"If you say so. But then, I've always been one to change horses in midsentence."

Wolfe's eyes narrowed. "There are alternatives, of course," he said with a sigh. "I could ignore you, you would continue prattling, and the atmosphere here would become strained. Or I could humor you by inquiring as to where you are attempting to shepherd the conversation. The risk in choosing the latter approach is that I might not relish the direction."

"That's a problem, all right," I conceded. "Let's assume, though, that despite the peril associated with the latter course, you decide to take it. That course itself has two options: One, that I discuss our finances first; the other, that I talk about what's really on my mind."

"I'll risk the latter," Wolfe said dryly, ringing for beer.

"Okay. Cherr-o-key is a soft drink, cherry flavored, or so I've been told—I've never had one." Wolfe made a face that registered his opinion of such a beverage. Undaunted, I went on to describe Lily's Super Bowl party and the Cherr-o-key commercial, and then related my conversations with Mills, including his appeal.

Wolfe snorted. "Unthinkable."

"Unthinkable that one advertising agency would steal the ideas of another?"

Wolfe poured beer into a tall glass from one of two bottles Fritz had brought in, then scowled as he watched the foam settle. "No, unthinkable that you would bring forth such a preposterous proposal."

"A lot of our jobs have begun with even more preposterous proposals."

"Pah."

"Pah yourself. All right, then, if that's going to be your attitude, here's something to munch on between grunts," I said, getting up and taking the two strides necessary to reach his desk. I dropped a single sheet of paper on his blotter and returned to my swivel chair. He picked the sheet up and read, his face expressionless.

"What you are reading is the story of three months of inactivity," I told him. "Our checking account balance is the lowest it's been in eight years. I know—I went back through the records this morning. Oh, and I also know, so don't bother to bring it up, that you've got some dandy investments that pay healthy dividends regularly. But even those—and I'll concede they are nice—aren't enough to keep you living in the manner to which you've grown accustomed. For instance, there's that damn bill for—"

"Archie!"

"Yes, sir?"

"You once said you despised industrial espionage cases. Clearly, that is what this appears to be, if one chooses to term advertising an industry."

"You're such a stickler for accuracy that I'm surprised at that statement. I never said I despised industrial espionage cases *en toto*—it was specifically the so-called business with that electronics outfit up in Westchester, the one with the goofy owner who thought the Commies were out to get him so he built fortifications all around—"

"I remember all too well!" Wolfe rumbled. "I also

recall that you whined incessantly about having to deal with the man."

"I didn't whine," I said with a sniff. "I merely was voicing my disapproval of our client's personality, mentality, morality, and lifestyle. You weren't exactly fond of him, either, as I recall. But you *did* like the color of his lettuce."

Wolfe scowled and began looking through the letters I'd typed. He started to sign the first one when I cut in.

"It won't work."

Wolfe set his fountain pen down deliberately and glowered at me, inhaled a cubic foot of the mixture we refer to as oxygen, and let it out slowly. "Twaddle."

"You think that by brushing me off, you can make this potential client—and me—go away."

"I can see Mr. Mills at three o'clock today," Wolfe said. "But—and mark me on this—I reserve the right to decline his appeal summarily, without supplying any reason whatever."

"What else is new?" I responded. "I'll call Mills."

Wolfe ignored me, of course, turning back to the letters. I had taken Round One on points, but I was damned if I was going to chortle, certainly not out loud. I pulled out Mills's business card and phoned the ad agency. After identifying myself, I was immediately put through to Mills.

"Goodwin! God, I was just getting ready to call you. Did you talk to Wolfe?"

"I did. Be here at three, and be prompt." I gave him the address.

"Then he'll take the case?"

"I didn't say that. But he will talk to you, which is

a beginning. By the way, that was a nice write-up you folks got in this morning's *Times*."

"Yeah, it was okay, especially after what's been going on. One more thing . . ." Mills paused, as if choosing his words. "I wonder if Wolfe would mind if my partners came too. Boyd and Sara are, well, *interested* just as much as I am, you know."

"Hold on." I cupped the speaker and swiveled to Wolfe. "Mills wants to include his partners in our palaver. There are two—a man and a woman."

He growled low in his throat which undoubtedly reflected his opinion of having members of the opposite sex in the office, then nodded grimly.

"Okay, bring 'em along," I said to Mills, "but only if they promise to wipe their shoes on our welcome mat." My anemic attempt at humor was rewarded with an anemic chuckle from Mills, who promised to be on time.

I hung up and turned back to Wolfe. "For the record, the partners' names are Boyd Lake and Sara Ryman. Would you like further information on either of them before they partake of your munificent hospitality?"

He set down his current book, *The Last Lion* by William Manchester, and picked up one of the pieces of correspondence I had left for him. "Archie, you will have to retype this letter to the gentleman in Wisconsin. You misspelled *Paphiopedilum* twice."

"Sorry, but I guess my mind must have been on other things—like the bank balance."

I got no reply, but then, I didn't expect one.

THREE

During lunch, which was Fritz's matchless bay scallops meunière with rice and creamed spinach, followed by crème caramel, Wolfe discoursed on how the various Western European countries' cultural differences and chauvinistic vanities would prevent there ever being a truly united Europe—in 1992 or ever. While he talked, I nodded, chewed, and swallowed.

When we were back in the office with coffee, I tried to shift the conversation to our soon-to-arrive guests, but Wolfe wasn't having any of that. "Archie, you pressured me to see Mr. Mills, and I agreed, albeit reluctantly. However, until he and his entourage arrive, I shall continue reading. I assume the orchid germination records have been updated."

"Is that a rhetorical question?" I snapped. I got no reaction, so I made a production out of tidying up my desk, using my long-handled brush to sweep the blotter and then using the electric pencil sharpener to put new points on a half-dozen yellow number twos.

"Must you continue with that infernal bobbery?" Wolfe said, setting his book down and ringing for beer.

"Just getting prepared," I said with a shrug and what Lily refers to as my choirboy smile, although I never was a choirboy. "The quality of my note-taking is directly proportional to the keenness of my pencil points." That was worth a huff from Wolfe. I started to huff back, but the ringing of the phone interrupted me. It was Lon, calling to say his advertising writer had no negative information of any kind about M/L/R. "He says they're a serious, hardworking bunch with a fine future," Lon said. "We should all get such good reviews." I thanked him and sat in silence staring at the cover of Wolfe's book until two-fifty-nine, when the front doorbell rang. I went to the hall and peered through the one-way glass in the door.

There were three of them, all right. Mills was in the center, flanked by a frowning, stocky, bearded specimen whose reddish hair—both pate and facial—had a good start on gray, and a slender brunette with a well-arranged face who didn't look any too cheerful herself. They both appeared to be about Mills's age, which is to say fortysomething, or maybe late thirtysomething.

"Right on time," I said brightly as I pulled the door open, thinking an upbeat approach might lighten up our visitors. It didn't.

"Archie Goodwin, this is Sara Ryman and Boyd Lake," Mills said as I did coat-hanging honors in the front hall.

I shook hands with Lake, who grunted, and then I turned toward Sara Ryman, who cocked her head. "You're not as tall as I thought you'd be," she said coolly and without smiling, smoothing the skirt of her well-tailored dove-colored suit. "Neither are you," I cracked as we walked down the hall toward the office. "By golly, even in heels, you can't be a hair over five-six." Still no smile.

I made introductions and got the trio seated, Mills in the red leather chair, the others in the yellow ones. Grimly, Mills explained that Boyd Lake was the agency's executive vice president for creative and Ms. Ryman was the executive vice president for art. After offering drinks—Mills and Lake each took Scotch on the rocks and the lady shook her head—Wolfe considered them without enthusiasm. "Mr. Mills," he said after a sigh, "Mr. Goodwin has of course given me an outline of your agency's problem, as it was elucidated to him when you met on Sunday. But I would like greater detail."

"Understood." Mills nodded, looking at his glass and then at his two glum partners. "Any place special you want me to begin?"

"You stated to Mr. Goodwin that on two occasions, advertising campaigns generated by your organization for a soft drink were stolen and used—"

"That's not quite accurate," Lake cut in, leaning forward. Mills hadn't mentioned that he was British. His accent was pure Dudley Moore. "Copied, *aped,* is a truer description."

Wolfe's gaze moved from Mills to Sara and back. "Would you both concur?"

"No question," Sara Ryman said sharply. "Somebody at Colmar and Conn found out what we were doing and lifted the ideas both times. But they gave them their own slight twists. They weren't complete steals—but close."

"Damned close!" Mills snapped and his partners nodded grimly.

Wolfe poured beer, watching the foam dissipate. "Describe the commercials," he said, "both your concepts and those your competitor developed."

"Boyd oversees all our creative output," Mills said. "He can give you the clearest rundown."

The Englishman leaned back, his stomach testing the strength of the thread holding his vest buttons. "The first one, that would have been when—in August, Sara?"

"July," she corrected curtly.

"July, right. Yes, it wasn't long after the Fourth. Anyway, we conceived a new Cherr-o-key campaign built around outdoor participation sports—team sports—played by both men and women. You know, volleyball, softball, touch football, that sort of thing. Our theme was 'The Cherr-o-key Crowd,' complete with a soft-rock song we commissioned. We had one of the most popular of the current young singers lined up, too. We got Foreman's blessing, we started in with the shoots, we—"

"Foreman?" Wolfe asked, eyebrows raised.

"Yes, Mr. Wolfe," Mills put in. "Acker Foreman. He's the sole owner of Cherr-o-key. It's a private company, and he's—"

"He's eccentric, as in cantankerous, not to mention obnoxious." Sara Ryman could sound acid when she wanted to. "He chews up ad agencies and spits them out. Hell, we're the fourth shop—no, make that the fifth—that he's had in the last ten years. Foreman's a goddamn sadist!"

"Now, now, Sara, you're talking about our meal-ticket, the man we love," Lake chided with a tight smile.

"Speak for yourself, Boyd," she fired back, not amused.

"Well, he *does* account for a damn sight more than half our billings," Lake responded with a wave of the hand.

"But he did accept your proposal for this outdoor sports campaign?" Wolfe, bless his heart, was trying to steer the discussion back on track.

"True," Sara conceded, "but only after grumbling about it and indulging in his usual nit picking."

Lake shrugged. "For him, that performance was actually pretty mild, wouldn't you say, Rod?"

"Indeed. Mr. Wolfe, Acker Foreman is a legend in the soft drink business; a self-made millionaire from Oklahoma, he's part Cherokee, or so he claims, which is where the name of the drink comes from. He's in his late seventies, and he's eccentric, to say the least. In recent years, he's become something of a recluse, but the guy's done damn near everything in his life, including oil wildcatting and construction. He even started an airline in the Southwest back in the forties, which he later sold to one of the big guys and made a fortune. The problem is, he's also a legend as a tough client, as Sara says. He can be hell to deal with, and he hates to spend money on advertising. As big as his brand is, it's woefully underadvertised, which we think has hurt it against AmeriCherry. Like every other agency he's had, we've tried to get him to spend more, but he just thinks all ad agencies are reckless and money-hungry. But then, we knew all that about him going in when we got the Cherr-o-key business two years ago."

"And seeing his major competitor come out with TV spots a lot like the ones he'd already okayed hasn't improved his disposition any," Lake offered. He and Mills exchanged a look I couldn't quite translate.

"Didn't I see Mr. Foreman's photograph in one of the newspapers—the *Gazette,* I believe—last week?"

"You did," Mills replied, finishing his Scotch. "He and one of his jerky sons were in court testifying. Some guy had brought suit claiming he had come up with a name similar to 'Cherr-o-key' for a soft drink years ago, but it was thrown out. It was really a nuisance suit, from the sound of it."

"How similar to your advertising was the work done for the competitor?" Wolfe asked.

Mills glanced at Sara. "Startlingly," he said. "Boyd just described our outdoor sports campaign. We had begun shooting the spots when AmeriCherry, they're the competitors, aired a one-minute commercial that showed a bunch of young men and women playing volleyball while a soft-rock group sang about 'the AmeriCherry crew—' "

" 'They're just like me and you,' " Sara sarcastically finished the couplet while Wolfe shuddered at the syntax.

"The lyrics exemplified the spot," Lake said. "It wasn't technically a very good piece of work. It looked like it had been thrown together."

"Hell, of *course* it was thrown together." Sara's face was white. "It had to be to beat us on the air. But it blew our campaign clean out of the water."

"Might this have been coincidental?" Wolfe asked.

Mills took a deep breath and crossed his long legs. "Unlikely, but conceivable—if this had happened only once. But as you know, there was a second time."

"This really cinched it," Lake said, picking up the narrative. "In October, we hit on a sweepstakes idea, we called it the 'Cherr-o-key Spree.' Now sweepstakes aren't exactly original, but this had a spin to it—it put us on the side of the angels, so to speak. Or rather, it would have if it had got off the ground."

"Just tell the story, Boyd," Sara grumbled.

"I'm getting to it, this takes time. Like most soft drinks, Cherr-o-key comes in cans, disposable bottles, and returnable bottles. We decided to score points with the environmentalists by making the returnable bottles more attractive to the consumer. Our sweepstakes vehicle was to have been the bottle caps on the returnable bottles only. You know, peel off the cork and win a prize—everything from a deck of playing cards or a case of Cherr-o-key to a new Buick or a trip to Aruba, that kind of thing.

"But," Lake said, pounding a fist into a fleshy palm, "we were going to make a big deal out of how we were stressing the use of our returnable bottles. And, Cherr-o-key, with much fanfare, was going to contribute a nickel to one of the major environmental organizations for every returnable bottle sold."

"Did Mr. Foreman like this plan?" Wolfe asked, draining his second beer.

"He was . . . lukewarm," Rod Mills said. "I think the idea of coughing up all that cash for both the prizes and the environment hit him in the gut. But we kept stressing how good it would make Cherr-o-key look.

With categories like soft drinks, where there's really no appreciable product difference, you've got to work to find an edge."

"He finally bought the program," Sara Ryman said, "but it was too late."

"You've got that right," Lake said, the American slang sounding strange piggy-backed onto his English accent. "Damned if AmeriCherry didn't come out with a bottle-cap game of its own while we were still on the drawing board—we hadn't even firmed things up with the environmental group yet. Their bottle caps had pictures of endangered species underneath the cork, and by collecting a full set, one could win prizes similar to the ones we'd planned, and also have a contribution made in their name to a wildlife fund. Needless to say, Foreman killed our campaign. God, he was livid."

Mills nodded glumly. "He summoned us to his office in Midtown and raised hell in the conference room for an hour. Said if we didn't find the 'goddamn leak,' as he called it, we were finished as his agency. Mr. Wolfe, we *know* there's a leak, but we haven't been able to find it. That's why we're here."

"Yet Mr. Foreman let you spend what apparently was a great deal of money on the extravagant commercial described to me by Mr. Goodwin?"

"The Super Bowl spot, yes. We did that in part to redeem ourselves with him."

"Were you successful?"

"So it seems," Mills said. "I haven't talked to Foreman since the spot ran—which was only yesterday—but I understand from one of his underlings that he was pleased. That doesn't let us off the hook, though. Just because AmeriCherry didn't steal our Super Bowl idea doesn't mean our leak has gone away. Or that Foreman has gotten soft."

"It may simply mean that he liked the creative."

"The creative *what?*" Wolfe asked.

"In advertising, creative can be a noun as well as a modifier," Mills explained.

Wolfe made a face at this desecration of the language. "Has Cherr-o-key's competitive position been damaged by the apparent pilfering of commerical ideas?"

Mills shook his head. "If you're asking if sales have suffered vis-à-vis AmeriCherry, it's really too early to tell. And we really may never know. Because of the huge volume each brand does, it's almost impossible to attribute rises and falls in sales to any single factor. Foreman's pride is hurt, though, to say nothing of his competitive nature. He hates AmeriCherry, and he hates to lose."

"And to say nothing of *our* competitive nature," Sara put in. "We hate Colmar and Conn, and we hate to lose, too."

"Hear, hear," Lake said, clapping twice.

Wolfe ignored the breast-beating. "When you begin planning a commercial or any other kind of advertising, how many people know the details?" he asked.

"That varies. At the beginning, maybe only three or four on the creative team are developing the strategy. But as the process moves along, the number by necessity increases. If it's a major campaign, and in our shop everything to do with Cherr-o-key is major, all the employees pitch in, including the clerical staff. Then with TV, there are all the suppliers. For instance, an outside production house actually shoots the spot.

And there's the talent, of course—that's the actors and actresses—plus representatives of the client who show up on the set during the shooting and generally do nothing more than get in the way."

Wolfe frowned. "In other words, an army."

"Of sorts," Mills said, grinning sheepishly.

"Who from Cherr-o-key attends these shootings?"

"Usually the old man and at least one of his sons, both of whom work for him and both of whom are frankly pains in the gluteus maximus."

"Why is that?"

"Basically because they're asses—Arnold is loud and crude, Stephen is less loud, and sullen. Plus they don't know squat about advertising, and they've never made the effort to learn. It's Dad's company, though, so if he doesn't object to their being around, who are we to complain? Especially because—barring a hostile takeover, which is unlikely given how closely held the operation is—those two clowns will be running the place some day."

"Not that it matters to us," Lake said wryly. "Before Old Acker departs this life, he'll probably have changed agencies at least three more times."

"True," Mills said, nodding. "We're just another in a long parade. And even if we were to outlast the old man, the sons would probably can us in a minute, the way we've gotten along with them."

"I take it there is animus between you?"

Sara moved uneasily in her seat. Mills laughed. "To put it mildly. Both of them—particularly Arnold—sound off when we make presentations. As I said before, they don't know a damn thing about advertising, but that doesn't stop them. Hell, a few months ago, when Boyd was showing Acker and sons storyboards for a proposed new TV spot, Arnold jumped up and said 'Dad, this stuff stinks.'"

"Now Rod, you're cleaning up Arnold's language," Sara chided with a tight smile.

"Okay, so he didn't say 'stinks,'" Mills answered. "But that brought Boyd out of the trenches and he told Arnold to stuff it."

"Things *were* a little tense that day," Lake chimed in. "I'm not sorry I popped off, though. After all, it resulted in Arnold storming out of the room in a funk. Acker didn't make any effort to stop him, though, and we ended up getting the commercial approved."

"Back to the business at hand; neither you nor your partners here have any idea who might be the conduit to the rival advertising agency?" Wolfe asked.

"God knows we've talked enough about it." Lake stroked his beard and toyed with his maroon knit tie. "And we've called in every one of our employees—we've got fifty-two in all, including ourselves—and grilled them as much as we could without totally undermining morale. Maybe I'm a Pollyanna, but I refuse to believe it's anyone on our payroll."

"Of course you're a Pollyanna, Boyd," Sara said with a hard-edged laugh, giving me a good look at her profile, which was worth a good look. "But admit it, as I've been saying for days, the mole almost has to be someone in the house. We used different outside contractors and talent for the two campaigns. The only people who knew how we were proceeding from the beginning on each of them were our own."

Wolfe readjusted his bulk and contemplated the two beer bottles and the empty glass in front of him. "It has been some weeks since Mr. Foreman issued his ultimatum, yet he continues to employ your agency. Has he regained some measure of equanimity?"

"Not really," Mills said, rubbing his chin. "It's just that even for him, it's a pain to change shops, although as you've heard, he's done that often enough through the years. He's still on our case—and on me particularly—to find the leak. In the meantime, though, we're expected to keep on generating creative for Cherr-o-key."

"And you are?"

"Mr. Wolfe," Mills said, "as I told Archie Goodwin, that damn drink is responsible for roughly five-eighths of our billings—sixth-three percent, to be exact. Our media billings for last year—what it costs to put advertising on the air and into print—were around thirty million, and something over eighteen mil of that is for Cherr-o-key. Likewise, they account for about five-eighths of our gross income, or almost three million of the four and a half million we brought in. We lose the account, and we start firing people up and down the line, to say nothing of what it would do to our image. Right now, we're working like crazy—particularly Boyd and Sara here—to develop a fresh new campaign. It's more than a little difficult to do that *and* to hunt down a spy in our midst at the same time."

"Has word of these two idea-thefts reached the press?" Wolfe asked.

"Amazingly, no," Mills replied, looking at his partners. "We've all been terrified for weeks that one of the trade papers or the *Times* or the *Gazette* would find out about it."

"They still might," Sara murmured darkly. "It would be one hell of a story."

"Another question," Wolfe said, eyeing the wall clock which told him his afternoon playtime with the orchids was only six minutes away. "How was the other agency able to produce its simulacra so quickly?"

"It wasn't so much that they were fast," Lake said, "but that we were working at a relatively leisurely pace. We had no reason to hurry, other than Foreman's usual impatience. After all, we didn't realize we were about to have our ideas lifted. Even after the TV commercial, which some of us thought was a coincidence, we weren't fully on our guard."

"*I* was," Sara retorted.

"All right, Sara, let the record show you were immediately suspicious," Lake said, snorting loudly and rolling his eyes. "You've reminded Rod and me of it often enough. Anyway, Mr. Wolfe, after round two, the bottle-cap fiasco, even those of us who are slower-witted and less perceptive than Ms. Ryman here realized that something nasty was going on."

"Have you now instituted internal security measures?" Wolfe asked.

"Well," Mills said, squaring his shoulders. "Here's what we're—"

"Pardon me, sir," Wolfe cut in, holding up a palm, "but I have an engagement. However, Mr. Goodwin will discuss this matter further with you."

"But . . . we haven't talked about fees or any other specifics—"

Wolfe was on his feet now, and moving around the desk. "Mr. Goodwin and I will confer later, and you will be apprised of my decision. Good afternoon."

All of them watched in puzzled silence as Wolfe propelled himself out of the office and into the hall, where his elevator awaited.

"That's it?" Mills said. "That's the end of our audience?"

"Hey, you've still got yours truly here," I grinned. "And believe me, I'm one hell of a good listener, a thorough interrogator, and a superlative note-taker. Now let's talk some more about what you're doing to find your Benedict Arnold."

FOUR

"Is that standard behavior for your employer?" Lake asked after we got resettled and they all had turned down an offer of liquid refreshments.

"Where my employer is concerned, there's no such thing as standard behavior. If you're asking if he's eccentric, the answer is a resounding yes—but then, all geniuses are eccentric, or so I've been led to believe. And with Mr. Wolfe, what you're buying is nothing less than genius."

"But we apparently haven't bought *anything* yet, given Wolfe's comment on the way out." Mills's forehead looked like a mountain range on one of those topographical maps. The fretfulness he had carried on Super Bowl Sunday had clearly settled on him again. This was one very troubled man.

"Let me worry about that. If I were a betting man, I'd give six-to-one that he'll take you on. I know him well enough to tell when he's interested."

"Hmm. He sure didn't seem all that interested to me." Sara Ryman folded her arms and tilted her chin up.

"Trust me. And tell me what you've done so far to

find the leak and prevent further ones. For starters you mentioned that you called in your employees."

They both turned toward Mills. The adman shifted in the red leather chair, cleared his throat, and pondered Wolfe's desk blotter before replying. "Well, that sure as the devil wasn't very productive. Like Boyd said, we brought all forty-nine others in—one at a time—and talked to them. There were always two partners in various combinations in the room during the conversations, and we tried to make the talks nonthreatening."

"How?"

"The three of us rehearsed it ahead of time, because we were so concerned about undermining morale. We told everyone, from secretaries to creative directors, the same thing: that we knew there had to be some kind of conduit, to use Mr. Wolfe's term, to Colmar and Conn, but that it didn't necessarily have to be an employee—it could be one of our suppliers. Which is in fact true."

"But unlikely," Sara put in crisply. I was beginning to like the lady, but I wished she weren't so shy about voicing her opinions.

"Not necessarily," Mills said. "As I've told you before, I tend to agree with Boyd that the spy isn't one of our own folks."

"You still *really* believe that?" Sara snapped.

"Look, for the moment, let's just stay with your meetings with the staff," I said to Sara, then turned back to Mills. "From the way you're talking, I assume none of them aroused your suspicions."

"Correct. We never came out with anything as bald as 'Did you leak our spots to C and C?' What we did was to ask each of them if they had any inkling whatever about who else—either with the agency or a supplier—might have done it. And no one had even the slightest idea."

"Or so they said," Sara injected.

"Miss Ryman, since you are obviously skeptical about the innocence of all of the agency's employees, do you care to nominate a culprit?" I asked.

She shook her head vigorously. "No, Mr. Goodwin, but the point I'm trying to make is that I don't think we've been exactly thorough in our own investigation. By the way, it's *Ms.* Ryman."

"Sara, that is precisely why we're here," Lake said through clenched teeth. "To seek the aid of experts in this sort of thing. We're simply a bunch of tinhorns when it comes to interrogation."

"*Greenhorns,* Boyd," Sara corrected, smirking.

A vein started to throb in Lake's neck.

"All right, so much for your interrogations," I said. "What about preventive measures? Or 'internal security measures,' to use Mr. Wolfe's terminology."

Now they all looked uncomfortable. Both Sara and Boyd turned toward Mills.

"To be honest, we haven't really done anything there," he said slowly. "Mr. Goodwin, as we've told you, our agency is young and small, but with a wonderful . . ."

"Spirit!" Sara proclaimed.

"Yes, spirit. And that's been one of our greatest strengths up to now. God, we've got this great camaraderie, you know?" Mills said, his voice rising. "Lord, half our employees are under, what—twenty-seven?—and they like the idea that we're a small band taking on the big guys. Not just with Cherr-o-key, although that's our plum, but with some other accounts, too. The point I'm trying to make is that we're worried—terrified—of doing anything to upset the chemistry we've got going. So we've been very delicate about all this."

"Besides the three of you, who in the agency is most intimately involved in the Cherr-o-key campaign?" I asked.

"First off, I'm really not that involved myself, except in an overseeing sort of way," Mills said. "Boyd, as the chief creative, and Sara, who's in charge of art, are our key people, along with Annie Burkett, an art director on the account."

"Not *an* art director, *the* art director," Sara said. "And despite her young age, one of the best in the business, if I do say so myself."

"Mr. Goodwin," Lake said with an exaggerated sigh, "let the record show that Annie Burkett, indeed a talent of the first order, was hired by Sara, who immediately saw her potential and acted accordingly."

"Duly noted. And you feel that Ms. Burkett is above reproach?"

"I think so," Lake said.

"I don't *think* so, I *know* so," Sara said, tossing a condescending look toward her bearded partner. Then she shifted to me. "What I mean is that I know her so well I can vouch for her without hesitation."

"And you're suggesting I can't?" Lake snarled, standing up, hands on hips.

"Children, children," Mills said with a weak smile. "Boyd, sit down; you've known Sara long enough to recognize when you're being needled."

"Huh!" the creative director gruffed, easing back into his chair and pouting. "Given the situation we're in, it seems to me we need to concentrate on the problem, not on needling each other."

"You're right, Boyd," Sara said quietly. Her face took on a softness I hadn't seen before. "I'm sorry. I guess I'm just tense from all this. I apologize."

"We're all tense," Mills conceded. "Mr. Goodwin, we sit before you, three frazzled partners with our nerve endings pathetically exposed. What else can we tell you?"

"You mentioned outside suppliers. I'd like to hear more about them."

"Of course. With rare exceptions, advertising agencies don't actually *make* TV commericals themselves. They develop the overall campaign for the product or service, and they may also conceive the specific commercial, but as I told you and Mr. Wolfe earlier, they use the services of a director and a production house—these are people outside the agency. Same with the talent—the on-camera people. These are of course not employees of the agency. You know, like those skydivers and singers in the Super Bowl spot."

"But most of these people obviously know enough about your commercial that they could tip somebody else off about it, right?"

They all nodded, looking like three mourners at an Irish wake. "But," Lake said, breaking the silence and waggling a finger in my direction, "anybody doing something like that takes a terrible risk. Ours is a small community, and if it ever got out that someone was so treacherous, he—or she—would be finished. People jump around so much that today's ally is tomorrow's competitor. And people talk a lot in our business, too. They're all gossips."

"Boyd is right," Mills said. "Not too many years ago, there was a situation where a copywriter leaked information about a campaign in hopes it would get him a job with the agency that handled a competing brand. But Agency B wasn't about to take him on; after all, if he ratted on one, he'd likely rat on another, especially for the right price. Anyway, the mole eventually got found out. He was fired by Agency A and the word spread."

"He never worked in advertising again," Lake added.

"What all of this seems to say is that nobody spilled the beans to Colmar and Conn," I said. We were getting nowhere fast. "Don't any of you suspect *anybody*?"

"Mr. Goodwin, in spite of all my comments, even I truly can't suggest anyone specific," Sara Ryman said. She seemed to be getting more human by the minute. "I feel like I know everybody in the agency well enough that I can't believe any one of them did it—or at least I don't *want* to believe one of them did it. We've got such a high degree of loyalty."

"Aha, now who's the Pollyanna?" Lake purred. Sara flushed.

"Look, I'm glad all three of you are so pleased with the crackerjack staff you've put together, but the inescapable truth is, someone, either in the agency or associated with it, is a spy."

"What do you suggest, maybe lie detector tests?" Lake sounded skeptical.

"No, that's absolutely unrealistic," I said. "One, at

best they're of questionable value; two, mass testing of your staff would *really* send morale into the basement; and three, you run the risk of some terrible publicity. After all, you know damn well that if you tried testing, it would get out, and then so would the fact that your ideas are being pilfered. To say nothing of the legal aspects of this kind of testing. Would any one of you like to be the one who tries to compel all your people to sit still for the tests?"

"All right, how *can* you and Wolfe help us?" Mills demanded, leaning back and setting his jaw.

"First, we're all going to be optimists and assume Mr. Wolfe will agree to take you on. I've already given you the odds on that. At some point, I'll want to visit your offices and talk to a number of people. For starters, each of you individually, then—"

"Why us again?" Sara snapped, brushing a stray strand of hair back from her forehead. "You're talking to us *now*."

"True, but I like one-on-one chats, too. Sometimes people remember things better in those situations."

"Meaning we'd say things privately that we wouldn't say in front of our partners?"

"Not necessarily. I just like individual consultations," I said with a smile. "Also, I'll want to talk to the woman you mentioned, Annie Burkett. And maybe some others involved in the Cherr-o-key stuff, too."

Mills nodded grimly. "That'll stir things up some, of course, but I suppose there's no avoiding that."

"Not if you have any hope of finding out what's going on. Also, what about your client himself? How many people at Cherr-o-key know in advance what's going to be in their commercials?"

"Oh God, d'you have to go to *them,* too?" Lake actually wailed.

"Of course he does, Boyd," Sara said. "Mr. Goodwin, right off the top, I can think of three people at Cherr-o-key who know about the spots almost from their inception—Acker Foreman and those two idiot sons. But they'd have absolutely no reason to spill it to their competitors."

"You're probably right," I conceded. "But I'll still want to talk to them at some point. Mr. Mills, you told me when we were at Lily's party that you hadn't asked anybody at Colmar and Conn about the leak, right?"

"Of course I haven't!" He jerked upright in the chair, looking irked. "I wouldn't give them the satisfaction."

"Somebody will have to, if we expect to find out who the mole is," I said evenly. "In fact, that may be the place to start, but I'll get to that. Who's their honcho?"

"Harlowe Conn." Lake pronounced the name as if it were contagious.

"The expression on Boyd's face pretty well captures the way all of us feel about the Gray Eagle," Sara volunteered. Her voice took on an edge again. "He's really a . . . oh, never mind—he's not worth wasting perfectly good profanity on."

"The Gray Eagle? He sounds like a national institution."

"That's what *he* thinks he is, too," Mills huffed. His hands formed fists so tightly that his knuckles went white. I made a mental note to poke into whatever history existed between Harlowe Conn and Rod Mills. "Unfortunately, he's got some justification. He's an authentic, gold-plated war hero—Korea. A Marine pilot. Shot down some incredible number of MIGs, got shot down himself, won the Medal of Honor or some such."

"You don't sound impressed," I said.

"Maybe that's because the man's such a pompous jackass, and a phony to boot. To say nothing of his management techniques and his business morality."

"I guess you two don't get together for drinks and cribbage very often, eh?"

Sara laughed softly. Mills shook his head vigorously. "He's a viper, and I'd tell you that even if he and his cash-rich agency hadn't tried to buy us out once."

"This gets more intriguing by the minute," I said. "That last nugget of information suggests all sorts of interesting possibilities."

"Meaning? Oh—I get it," Mills said, slapping his forehead lightly. "Pardon my denseness. You think that because we wouldn't sell out to him, Conn has decided to get even with us by ripping off our ideas?"

"Sounds like one possibility."

"Well, that might be the case—the guy's sleazy enough, despite his hero's persona and that phony statesmanlike bearing," Mills said grimly, "but he couldn't do it without some help."

"Okay," I said, straightening up and stretching my arms, "here's how it looks to me: Someone who doesn't like your agency, or maybe one of you personally, or someone looking to make some quick and dirty money, decides to let your competitors know in advance the content of some of your advertising. That could—"

Sara sniffed. "Now tell us something we *don't* know."

"Just hold on for a minute—I'm not done. Class hasn't been dismissed," I said. Sara glared at me. Her eyes were really an extraordinary color. I made another mental note to decide later whether they were blue or green. "What I started to say was, that person—whether greedy or holding a grudge—could be with your agency, he could be with Cherr-o-key, he could be with one of your suppliers, or he could even be somebody who recently left your agency. Now that's one hell of a lot of people we're talking about. But to be successful in his perfidy, he—or maybc it's she—also would need to have an eager recipient of the information at Colmar and Conn, and probably a recipient who's willing to pay for it."

"Perfidy—now *there's* a word I haven't heard since university," Lake said approvingly.

"That's what comes of my being around Mr. Wolfe for so long. Anyway, I'd attack this whole business by going to your competitors first, because you're likely to get to the truth sooner that way. It's simply mathematics; you're dealing with a single institution at that end of the chain. At least one person there—probably high up—*has* to know where the leak is coming from."

Mills massaged the back of his neck with his hand. The man looked like he hadn't slept in a month. "Even if we were to go to them, which I'm not sure I'm prepared to do, you're assuming a lot by expecting that they will tell us a damn thing. More likely, they'll laugh in our—or your—face."

"I don't agree," I told him. "If this were to get out into the media, they'd look bad—probably worse than you would."

"You're suggesting threatening them with exposure?" Sara looked doubtful.

I raised one eyebrow. "Why not? How do you think they'd react to that?"

"They would probably call your bluff; then where would we be?"

"It's not entirely a bluff. For instance, the *Gazette* would be tickled pink to know about all this. But even without bringing them in, I think going to C and C is a chance worth taking. And face it, you're going to have to take *some* chances to get to the heart of the puzzle."

"This is all interesting, but right now, it's academic," Mills said. "I mean, your Mr. Wolfe hasn't even agreed to take us on yet. And if he does, we don't have the vaguest what his fee will be."

"The good news is that he will accept the challenge, or I wasn't born on a farm near Chillicothe in the great and sovereign state of Ohio. The bad news is that he doesn't come cheap. The other good news is that once on a case, he gets results."

The partners exchanged what I would describe as hopeful glances. "So what next?" Lake asked, turning to me and spreading his hands, palms up.

"I talk to Mr. Wolfe when he descends from the plant rooms at six. Once I get an answer, you'll hear from me within minutes."

Mills breathed deeply and loudly. "What choice do we have at this point?" He looked at his partners. Lake shrugged; Sara nodded. Mills turned back to me. "All right, we'll wait for your call. You guarantee we'll get an answer today?"

"I'll do everything in my power. That's not a guarantee, but it's the next best thing."

They rose together and filed out of the office, still looking as if they'd been at a wake. I followed them down the hall and helped Sara Ryman on with her fur coat while the men wrestled theirs on. She turned to me with something approaching a smile and started to say thank you, but checked herself. Still, that was progress.

FIVE

When I got settled back in the office, I looked over my shorthand and mentally played back Wolfe's conversation with the partners. Based on what I had observed, it appeared that one of Mills's roles in the threesome was as peacemaker and smoother of ruffled feathers. Boyd Lake and Sara Ryman obviously had flinty sides, and they seemed to relish baiting each other. Was this merely the good-natured banter of creative types, or—just maybe—symptomatic of a deep-seated mutual dislike?

My money was on the latter, but that was for Wolfe to dope out. After all, he's the resident genius, and as such the one who plumbs the darkest recesses of psyches. I'm only the errand boy, office boy, court jester, and resident scold. For the next hour, I put on my office-boy hat, balancing the checkbook and entering an article into the PC that Wolfe had worked up in longhand for an orchid growers' journal. And yes, I made damn sure I spelled *Paphiopedilum* correctly this time. When he came down from the plant rooms at six, the orchid essay—six typo-free double-spaced pages—had been printed out by yours truly and was neatly stacked on his blotter.

After getting his bulk settled behind the desk and ringing for beer, Wolfe leafed through the piece, grunting occasionally.

"Everything in order?" I asked. Another grunt, while he reread it.

I tried again. "Would you like a report on what transpired after your four o'clock ascension?" Fritz entered bearing a tray with the standard order: two chilled bottles of Remmers and a pilsener glass. Wolfe nodded his thanks, opened one of the bottles, dropped the cap into his center drawer, poured, and watched the foam settle.

"Confound it, go ahead, or you'll badger me right up until dinnertime," he grumbled, taking his first gulp of beer in more than two hours.

"Yes, sir." I fed him a verbatim account without glancing at my notes, which is a snap. After all, this had been a mere sixty-seven-minute session, and I've been known to spew back hours' worth of gabbing, word for word. I don't mean to boast—it's just a faculty I have—an "anomaly," Wolfe calls it.

Anyway, he leaned back with his fingers interlaced over his center mound while I performed my anomaly, including the parts where I did everything but guarantee the partners that Wolfe would ultimately accept the case. After I finished, he sat with his eyes closed for all of two minutes; when he resurfaced, he refilled his glass.

"Well, what now?" I asked.

Wolfe shifted his bulk. "Get Mr. Mills on the telephone," he decreed.

I had the agency's number on my pad, along with a notation that Mills would be in the office until at least seven. After I dialed, Wolfe picked up his instrument. On the third ring, the boss himself answered, and I stayed on the line.

"Mr. Mills, this is Nero Wolfe. I am calling to inform you that I agree to undertake your problem. My fee, which is not negotiable, is fifty thousand dollars, plus expenses. One-half payable immediately in the form of a cashier's check."

I could hear Mills wheeze. "That's . . . pretty steep," he said, clearing his throat.

"So it is, sir," Wolfe replied evenly. "Once again, refresh me as to how much the soft drink's business is worth to your agency."

Mills let several seconds pass before answering. "Point taken. I will of course have to discuss this with my partners before giving you an answer."

"Of course. Assuming you accept the terms, Mr. Goodwin will require access to all of your employees and suppliers, although it may not be imperative for him to speak to each one of them. It would be preferable if he operated incognito, but regrettably, he has at least in a limited way become a public figure and would soon be identified. Therefore, we have no option but to conduct the inquiry in the open."

"I understand," Mills said stiffly. "Is there anything else before I talk to Sara and Boyd?"

"Yes. Mr. Goodwin will almost surely find it necessary to pay a visit to Colmar and Conn as well."

"As you know, my partners will love hearing that."

"Just so," Wolfe said, ignoring the sarcasm. "After you consult them, you may inform Mr. Goodwin as to your decision." Mills grumpily said that he would and we all hung up.

"Well, you sure used 'Mr. Goodwin' often enough in that little chat," I said. "Which is okay, I suppose, but what about this 'in a limited way' stuff? Here I thought I was a full-fledged public figure in this vibrant and throbbing metropolis, a pop-culture icon not unlike yourself."

This time the deep breath came from Wolfe, who fixed me with one of his this-conversation-is-over glares before burrowing back into *The Last Lion.*

"Don't you wonder whether Mills and Company will hire you?" I said to the cover of the book. "Aren't you at least a little bit curious?"

Wolfe put down the volume and raised his shoulders a half-inch before lowering them. "Archie, you pride yourself on your ability to set odds on a variety of occurrences. Now I shall set some: I give you four-to-one that Mr. Mills calls within the next thirty minutes to accept my proposal. Actually, I am being generous; he is likely to telephone within fifteen—"

Wolfe was stopped by the ring of the phone, which I answered. "All right, Mr. Goodwin, Mills/Lake/Ryman agrees to the fee, although I have to tell you in all honesty that I think it's fairly outrageous." It was Boyd Lake, and he sounded exhausted.

"You'll get your money's worth, Mr. Lake," I told him. "What time do all of you get to the office in the morning?"

"It varies—I'm usually here by eight-forty-five, and so is Sara. Rod frequently is in before that—we tend to put in some long days. Most of the rest arrive between eight-thirty and nine, depending on what they're working on."

"I'll be there at eight-thirty tomorrow," I said. "Who should I ask for?"

"Rod, I suppose, although I know you'll be seeing all of us. He would have rung you back just now himself, but he's putting out a fire. Angry client, you know?"

"By any chance named Acker Foreman?"

The Englishman managed a weak laugh. "No, not this time, thank God. This is small stuff by comparison. But when any of our clients are upset, they always ask to talk to Rod, for which Sara and I are eternally grateful. He's a master at diplomacy. We'll look for you here tomorrow morning."

"Fine. And I assume a cashier's check for twenty-five thousand dollars will be waiting for me?"

Lake muttered something to the effect that it would. After I hung up, I turned to Wolfe, who leaned back and considered me through lidded eyes, the folds in his cheeks deepening. For him, that's the equivalent of an ear-to-ear grin.

"Don't get too smug," I said. "As you heard, that wasn't Mills who called."

"The effect is the same."

"All right, then be smug, if it makes you happy. We've still got twenty-two minutes before we get to attack Fritz's flounder with cheese sauce. How about some instructions regarding my visit tomorrow to the wonderful world of the hyperbolic sales pitch and the high-powered sell?"

That quickly erased his smugness; work or even the thought of it invariably sobers him. He drained the glass of half its beer, presumably to recharge his batteries. "Your notebook," he said sharply.

SIX

Tuesday morning after breakfast, I rechecked the address Mills had given me for the agency. It was down near the Battery, so I left the house a little after eight and flagged a taxi on Ninth Avenue. The cabbie zigzagged his way south and east, dropping me in front of a nondescript two-story brick building on Fletcher near South Street Seaport. Its architecture was early warehouse, but the brilliantly polished brass plate next to the front door with the words MILLS/LAKE/RYMAN on it proclaimed that I was at the right place.

My watch read eight-twenty-nine as I walked into the small lobby, which instantly dispelled all images of a warehouse. So did the vision behind the semicircular receptionist's desk. "May I help you?" she said softly with a practiced smile. The movement to brush a curl of butterscotch hair from her cheek was equally rehearsed.

"Sounds good to me. I'm here to see Mr. Mills," I said, letting her see that my teeth had been polished last week.

"Your name please?"

I pronounced it, and she picked up the orange

phone, which perfectly matched the color of an abstract tapestry on the wall behind her. "Yes, he's expecting you," she said, hanging up and putting her smile on automatic pilot again. "Up the steps and all the way down to the left, as far as you can go."

I thanked her and climbed one flight of carpeted stairs, emerging on an upper floor that had fluorescent lighting and cubicles separated by white, five-foot-high partitions. I walked down a long corridor to an open area where another vision, this one wearing dark hair and a dark green blouse, sat behind a white desk. "Ah, you are Mr. Goodwin," she said in a voice that made me want to hear her talk some more. And she knew how to make a smile seem genuine, too. "Please go right on in." She gestured toward one of two doorways behind her.

Mills's office was smaller than I had expected. It was a corner room all right, and with windows on two sides, but given the view from them, so what? I figured he must be a railroad buff, because the walls were covered with splashy Art-Deco-style posters that looked like they came from the 1920s. They had chic, smug-looking women on them and advertised trains serving London, Paris, Venice, and a bunch of other towns I never heard of. As I walked in, Mills was on the phone behind a cluttered desk that was really a table. He was in his shirtsleeves, tie loosened, and wearing bright green suspenders. The dark crescents under his eyes had deepened. "Okay, I *know* that," he said into the receiver, motioning me to a chair facing him. "Yeah, all right . . . I'll take care of it, I'll tell him. Yes, yes, I've gotta go. Good-bye." He hung up and shook his head. "Goddamn prima donna. That was one of the commercial producers we use—he's good, but he thinks he knows everything and he doesn't get along with Boyd, who knows what our clients want. Somehow, I always end up in the middle. Enough of that. I see you found our little corner of Gotham. Want some coffee? Lisa can get you a cup—high-octane or decaf."

"No thanks, I've had my quota for the morning. It's been years since I was in an advertising agency. The last time was up on Madison Avenue."*

"The business has changed in New York." Mills leaned back and slipped his thumbs under his green suspenders. "Almost nobody's on Madison any more—just a couple, including our fat cat buddies, Colmar and Conn. It's just too damn expensive. A lot of the shops have moved west of Fifth Avenue or south, some of them, like us, way south. The big guys are pretty well scattered, and the little guys—again like us—could never afford Madison Avenue rents, anyway. But this is perfect." He freed his thumbs and made a sweeping gesture with one arm. "Rehabbed building, used to be a small chemical company, office and labs and a shipping department, that sort of thing. Nothing fancy, as you can see. We don't own the building, of course, but we got ourselves a good deal on the lease. Oh, and before I forget it, here's your first installment, as requested." He picked up an envelope and handed it to me. I opened it to find a cashier's check for twenty-five big ones, made out to Nero Wolfe.

"Thank you," I told him. "Have you been in this building since the agency began?"

"Practically. The three of us met while we were all

*_Before Midnight_, by Rex Stout.

working for one of the bigger agencies in Midtown—Bradley-Watts, you've probably heard of them. Anyway, we got to know each other pretty well, and we—Boyd, Sara, and I—started talking about how it would be to have our own shop. This seemed particularly logical because of our different skills. Although I was on the creative side early in my career, I'm really more a sales guy, a 'Mr. Outside' used to dealing with clients, most of whom are pretty demanding. Boyd and Sara are creatives who don't care if they never see a client. Boyd's a copywriter, one of the best anywhere, despite his weakness when it comes to the American vernacular."

"As in tinhorns?"

Mills chuckled. "Yeah, as in tinhorns. And Sara's strengths are in the art and graphics areas. So we felt we had a good balance, for starters. And our goals were modest. Nothing huge, mind you, just a nice-sized operation with only a few clients—but good ones."

"And, presto! You did it."

"Yes and no," Mills said, leaning back and letting his arms dangle. "The 'yes' is that right now we're close to the size that we originally visualized. The 'no' is that we never wanted to have one client dominate our billings the way Cherr-o-key does."

"So why did it happen?" I asked.

Mills raised his arms as if each hand held a hundred-pound barbell, then let them drop again. "Why does it ever happen? Greed, of course, the bald, unadulterated variety. When we first pitched Foreman two years ago, we didn't figure we had a prayer of getting any of the Cherr-o-key business. Hell, we knew the guy was a bastard to deal with, but we also knew what kind of money went with the business. And I guess you could say we were like every other agency that's taken him on: We thought we could tame him—will him to our way of thinking, you know? What folly."

"Hubris, as Mr. Wolfe would say."

"I know the word, and Wolfe's right. Anyway, now you're pretty well up-to-date."

"Pretty well. Anybody here ever work for Colmar and Conn?"

Mills leaned forward and frowned, shaking his head. "I'm proud to say no to that. And nobody who's over there ever worked here, either. So there's no—" He stopped in midsentence, looking over my shoulder toward the doorway. I turned to see Sara Ryman standing with another woman, and neither of them looked as if they'd just won the lottery.

"Rod, sorry to break in, but Boyd hasn't showed up yet, and besides, Annie has something you need to hear—and Mr. Goodwin, too." She didn't bother to favor me with a glance. So much for detente.

Mills got to his feet and introduced me to Annie Burkett, the art director Sara had yesterday referred to as "one of the best in the business." I got a firm handshake and a questioning look from a face in which all the parts came together nicely, from a straight nose, wide gray eyes, and russet hair to cheekbones that belonged on the cover of a fashion magazine.

"I haven't told Annie why he's here," Sara said to Mills, still ignoring me. I began to see why her skills didn't lie in client relations. "Maybe you should, before she starts."

"Absolutely," Mills said as the women slipped into

chairs on my right. "Archie Goodwin works for Nero Wolfe, the private detective, and the agency has just hired Wolfe to help us with our, uh . . . *problem* with Cherr-o-key."

"Which is also why Annie's here," Sara contributed.

"Go ahead," Mills told the young woman. "Goodwin knows all about this mess. Now what's up?"

Annie Burkett ran a hand through her hair and studied me. "Well, I just told Sara that I got a call last night—it was about eight-thirty—from a friend who works for . . ."

"Colmar and Conn." Sara, ever helpful, finished the sentence for her. "It's all right, Annie. I told you there's nothing illegal about having acquaintances up there."

"Oh, I know. It's just that right now they're a dirty word around here—"

"As they damn well should be," Mills muttered.

"Yes, that's true." Annie nodded. "Anyway, this friend—his name is Andy Swartz—called and told me he wanted to see me. He sounded awfully upset. I asked him what it was all about, and he said he didn't want to talk about it on the phone. He asked if I could meet him that night for a drink. I told him I was just leaving for a class—I take French two nights a week—but that, yes, I could see him. I asked again what he wanted to see me about. All he would say was that it had to do with 'the cherry drink business.' " Her voice had a soft Southern tinge.

"Miss Burkett, were those his exact words?" I asked.

"I think he said, 'We need to talk about the cherry drink business.' "

"That's all?"

She turned her palms up. Her cheeks flamed. "That's all. He sounded pretty bent out of shape. I told him I'd meet him at eight tonight at Toohey's, that's a place on Bleecker in the Village."

"I know where it is. How do you happen to know this Andy Swartz?"

"He used to see a friend of mine who worked in the promotion department at *Flame and Flair* magazine. Sometimes when I had a date, we'd all go out together. We'd joke a lot about being competitors in the advertising business."

"What does Swartz do at Colmar and Conn?"

"He's a creative director, and a very good one."

"That's true," Mills said. "He's young, but he's won a batch of awards already."

"Does he call you often?" I asked Annie.

"Why, *no,*" she replied, eyes wider than usual. "In fact, I was surprised to hear from him. I hadn't even seen Andy in, oh . . . a while."

"Have you ever dated him?"

"No."

"Does he call you often?"

"This was the first time," she said, exasperation edging into her voice.

"Any idea why he chose last night to call you?"

She shook her head vigorously. "No, I—"

"Mr. Goodwin, it's obvious," Sara Ryman said coldly. "This Swartz has some kind of information about how our work is getting leaked to C and C. He's apparently an honest guy, and since Annie's the only person he knows here, he wants to tell her about it."

"Are you sure that Miss Burkett is the only one at this agency that he knows?" I asked. "As Mr. Lake said yesterday, the advertising community is a small one."

Mills rapped a pen against his desk. "I'm afraid I can't answer that. What about you two?"

"*I* certainly don't know him," Sara said.

Annie rubbed her cheek. Her gray eyes refused to meet mine. "If Andy has any other friends here, I'm not aware of it. And I don't think I've ever heard anyone here mention him."

"Well, I'm sure as hell anxious to find out what it is he wants to tell you." Mills dropped the pen and hooked his thumbs under his suspenders again. "What are your thoughts, Mr. Goodwin?"

"I don't have any more clue than you do about what Swartz wants to tell Miss Burkett. However, I do feel it would be a good idea if I showed up at Toohey's tonight, too."

"But Andy might not open up to me with someone else around," Annie said, leaning forward in her chair and looking earnest.

"Agreed, but he won't know I'm around. I've been in Toohey's, I know the layout. I assume you'll sit in a booth—there's lots of them there, and Swartz is going to want privacy. In the immortal words of Miles Archer, 'You don't have to look for me; I'll see you all right.' When Swartz unloads whatever it is that's bugging him, you give a signal for me to come over, say a dropped napkin, and we'll talk some more. Even Mr. Wolfe will tell you I'm pretty fair at worming information out of people who may not want it wormed out of them."

"Who's Miles Archer?" Annie said, looking puzzled.

Sara folded her arms disapprovingly. "Oh, he's a

character from *The Maltese Falcon.* Sounds to me like our Mr. Goodwin has been reading too many detective stories, or the movies made from them."

"By golly, you've got me," I told her. "And here I threw that reference in just to impress you."

Sara sniffed. "You're a parody of a detective. I think we can do nicely without your advice."

Once again Mills ran interference for his touchy partner.

"I don't agree," he said. "I like the idea of Goodwin being there tonight. Like he said, he's had a lot of experience getting people to talk, and Swartz might tell Annie only part of the story. Goodwin may be able to wring more out of him. Besides, I'd feel better if somebody else was around, in case Swartz . . . well, *does* something."

"Oh, God, you men all come out of the same mold," Sara grumped. "You've been exposed to too damn many James Bond movies. What do you think the guy's going to do, pull a gun—no, make that a 'gat'—on Annie?"

"Okay then, let's leave it to her to decide," Mills said, turning to Annie. "Do you want Goodwin there tonight, or not?"

The shy gray eyes studied me again. Then, for the first time, she smiled, if only slightly, revealing two dimples. "Okay, I . . . yes, I guess that would be a good idea. I mean, I'm not afraid of Andy, although I agree that Mr. Goodwin would have a better chance of finding extra things out. But . . ." She looked at me questioningly.

"Yes?"

"You wouldn't get *rough* or anything like that, would you?"

I suppressed a smile. "No, I wouldn't get rough, Ms. Burkett. That's really not my style, unless of course I'm treed or backed into a corner. And I don't expect that to happen tonight."

"I don't either," she said, smiling again. "Although to be honest, I am kind of nervous about this."

"Don't be," I reassured her. "Before I leave, give me a quick description of Swartz."

"Well, he's not all that tall—maybe two, three inches shorter than you are, probably three. Black hair, real curly, and it partly covers up his ears. Round face. Sometimes he wears glasses, the kind without rims."

"Build?"

"About average. He's not fat, but not real skinny either," she said.

"How old?"

"About thirty-two, I think, but to me, he looks a little younger."

"Okay. Remember that you may not be able to spot me tonight, but I promise I'll be where I can see you. And when you think Mr. Swartz has said all he's going to say and you're ready for me to make it a threesome, drop your napkin, or give it a good shove off the table. I guarantee that I'll be standing next to you less than fifteen seconds after it flutters to the floor."

I couldn't resist tossing that last bit in, strictly for Sara Ryman's benefit. She obviously had visions of me sitting up nights reading Chandler and Hammett and studying Sean Connery's stalking tactics and mannerisms and saloon demeanor on the VCR.

Who am I to disillusion her?

SEVEN

I spent the rest of the morning moving through the M/L/R offices and meeting staff members, who looked at me with expressions varying from curiosity to suspicion and downright hostility. Mills escorted me around, introducing me as "Archie Goodwin, who with Nero Wolfe is helping us look into our problem with Cherr-o-key." To show I was working, I went through the motions of asking a few questions here and there, getting suitably bland answers for my efforts. Nobody I asked said they knew Swartz, although most of them had heard of him.

Lake called in sick. Otherwise, the operation seemed fully staffed. I looked over a few shoulders, and in one case saw a storyboard for a commercial that a bearded art director named Berg assured me would "revolutionize the way dog food is marketed for the next decade." To my knowledge, that commercial never made it to the air, for whatever reasons. Maybe the world isn't ready for Dalmatians spouting Shakespeare, although the way Berg described it to me, it somehow made sense.

The atmosphere in the agency was freewheeling,

to say the least. Attire varied wildly—everything from ragged jeans and sweatshirts and tank tops to three-piece suits and pleated skirts. Same with the offices and work spaces. Decor was clearly an individual matter. Some walls were adorned with oils Lily would have been proud to hang in her apartment; others were painted in wild striped and swirl patterns or plastered with movie posters and bamboo screens and enlarged newspaper cartoons. And there was the artist whose cubicle had three parakeets in cages. When I asked Mills if the chirping wasn't a distraction, the response was, "Hell no, he's been living like that for years, at a half-dozen agencies. Wouldn't have it any other way. Says it soothes him while he works." I wondered what Wolfe's reaction would be if I brought three parakeets home and let them soothe me in the office.

By eleven-thirty, I felt I had got about all I was going to out of the M/L/R offices, and that included one-on-one conversations with Mills and Sara Ryman. Neither of those powwows shed much light, other than my confirming what I already suspected: that Sara indeed wasn't overly fond of Boyd Lake. "He's a brilliant copywriter," she told me when I asked about his strengths, "but his people skills are terrible. I know this is going to sound like ethnic stereotyping, but to me, Boyd is a typical Englishman—witty and bright, yes, but sardonic, cold, abrupt with people to the point of rudeness. He's a hard person to like."

"And you obviously don't like him."

She drummed a pencil on her desk blotter and smiled tightly, taking a deep breath. "I respect his abilities—and most important, I'm glad he's part of this agency. How's that?"

"Very diplomatic," I said with a smile of my own, and not a tight one. I thanked her for her time and excused myself.

Before leaving the agency, I dropped by to see Annie Burkett, whose own tiny office was downright conservative compared with most of the others, the only wall decoration being a framed photograph of the Golden Gate Bridge, shrouded in fog. I got a more detailed description of Swartz from her and confirmed that I would be in Toohey's at eight, which brought a somber nod. "Just be yourself tonight," I said in my warmest and most reassuring tone, but all that brought was a second unsmiling nod.

I got back to the brownstone just before noon. "Top of the morning," I said to Wolfe, who was entrenched at his desk with beer and book. "Anybody been looking for me?"

He grunted a no, but I wasn't about to let that slow me down, and I proceeded to relate the morning's activities. He reluctantly set his book down and leaned back, eyes closed, as I gave him the fill-in. When I got to the part about Annie Burkett and Toohey's bar, he grimaced and made a growling sound that I've never been able to imitate.

"What's the matter?" I asked. "I was using my intelligence, guided by experience, just as you have always instructed me to. Are you suggesting that I shouldn't go tonight?"

"No, confound it, you should go," he said, lifting his shoulders a full half-inch and letting them drop. "I assume you will take a gun?"

In Wolfe's view, any venture beyond the walls of

the brownstone, however brief, is extremely perilous, especially if it involves riding in a motorized vehicle. And to him, the peril increases geometrically if the trip may involve violence, although he always assumes I can handle all forms of combat short of nuclear missiles. I vowed that I would carry a firearm to Toohey's and asked if he had instructions.

"None for the moment, other than that you exercise good judgment." I thanked him for that nugget of wisdom and we went into the dining room to tackle Fritz's incomparable meatloaf while Wolfe speculated on what might have occurred had Churchill's father been American and his mother British instead of the reverse.

I spent the balance of the afternoon immersed in general bookkeeping, including an overhaul of the orchid germination records, which Wolfe had been on my case about for the last two weeks. I had to skip dinner because of my appointment, but Fritz, as ever concerned about my nutrition, promised to set a portion of the shish-kebab aside for me, and I thanked him profusely. Having visited Toohey's once before—with Saul Panzer, who had been keeping watch on a commodities trader who drank there—I knew the dress was eclectic, and I didn't want to stand out. I decided on my light brown herringbone sportcoat, dark brown slacks, and a white shirt with a red-and-white striped tie that Lily says makes me look rakish. As I recalled from my previous visit, Toohey's is loaded with rakes.

Saying good-bye to Wolfe, who was of course at his desk reading and getting ready to consume shish-kebab, I walked out the front door at seven-twenty-five to find that snow had begun falling. I went east all the way to Seventh Avenue before I found a cab. The driver, who sounded exactly like ex-Mayor Koch and said he was an NYU sociology graduate, wanted to talk about the sorry state of the New York public schools. He didn't get a lot except "yeahs" and "nos" out of me, but that didn't stop him.

Toohey's is on Bleecker just off MacDougal, in an old building that looks seedy from the second floor up. But the owner of the bar, presumably somebody named Toohey, had given the storefront a facelift—new brick-work, picture windows, oak double doors with old-fash-ioned handles and leaded windows, and one of those wooden country-inn-style signs hanging out over the sidewalk proclaiming this as "Toohey's Public House, Est. 1973." I paid the driver, who was still loudly mak-ing a point about the school system, and saw through the big windows that the place was beginning to fill up.

The interior looked the same as when I'd been there with Saul four years earlier: An island bar was just inside the front door to the left, with booths along the wall on the right and two more seating areas in the rear, each with booths. The nice thing was that from a stool on the far left side of the bar, I could see all the booths both in the main room and the two back seating areas and still remain inconspicuous. And the cut of the herringbone sportcoat was such that nobody could tell I was wearing a shoulder holster that had a Marley dozing in it.

Annie Burkett hadn't arrived yet, and there was only one man sitting alone in a booth, but he didn't come anywhere near matching her description of Swartz. I settled back with a Scotch-and-water and waited. At two minutes to eight, she walked in and peered briefly into the darkness at the bar, but if she was trying to find me, it was no good: I was well shielded by the guy on my right, who looked as if he could have played middle linebacker for the Jets sometime in the not-very-recent past.

She slid into a booth and gave a drink order to a waitress, looking nervously toward the door every few seconds. Each time it swung open, she tensed, but nobody joined her. She nursed her draft beer for twenty minutes, and I coaxed my Scotch right along with her, finally draining it and asking the bartender for a glass of water. I gave myself until eight-thirty. When the big hand of my watch finally covered the six, I walked over to the booth where Annie had been fidgeting.

"Hi. Seems like you've been stood up," I said.

"Oh, you *are* here," she said with a sigh that my vanity told me indicated relief. Then she crumpled a cocktail napkin. "I don't get it. I was positive he'd be here."

"You have his phone number?"

She flushed. "I think it's in the book."

"Fine. Let's use the pay phone, then, and find out why he got shy all of a sudden. I'll treat." I handed her a quarter. The phone book listed an Andrew Swartz on Charlton, which Annie said was his street. She dialed and after almost a half-minute turned to me with raised eyebrows. "No answer. He must have changed his mind, or else he had to work late."

"Looks that way. But as long as we're in the neighborhood, let's stop by his place. Hell, Charlton's only about a five-minute walk from here, and the night air will do us good after all this wanton debauchery."

Annie gave me a quizzical look. "Why do that, Mr. Goodwin? We already know he's not home."

"One, I answer to Archie, and two, maybe he'll have gotten home by the time we arrive there. Come on."

She let me help her on with her coat, but she clearly wasn't enamored of the idea of pursuing Swartz. "Look," I told her after I'd settled both checks and we were out on the sidewalk, "you don't want to end the evening still in suspense about what he wanted to see you about, do you? When I was growing up, my Aunt Clara always told me all women were imbued—and that's the word she used—with boundless curiosity, although I suppose now that would be seen as a sexist remark, right?"

"Well, it is fairly sexist," she said, arching an eyebrow nicely. "But if you swear your aunt said it . . ."

"Hope to die," I told her, raising my right hand in the oath-taking position.

She laughed, letting me see both dimples. "All right, maybe I am just slightly curious. Lead the way, sir—make that Archie."

The sky was clear now, the snow flurries having stopped, and there was no wind. It was one of those fine midwinter nights when the New York air smells truly fresh and clean. She hooked her arm in mine, and I like to think we looked as natural together as the other couples we passed on the lively sidewalks of Greenwich Village.

Andy Swartz's building was a trim four-story brick job that looked as if it had undergone a facelift in the last few years. Trees had been planted in front, and the tiny front yard had been completely bricked. We walked up six steps to the door and went into the small entrance hall, which had eight mailboxes. "A. Swartz" occupied Apartment 1-Rear. I rang the buzzer, getting no reply. I tried it again with the same result.

"All right," I said to Annie. "It's time for you to go home. Where do you live?"

She looked at me through narrowed hazel eyes. "Why?"

"Where do you live?"

"About a mile from here, over in SoHo. Again, why?"

"Let's find you a cab," I told her, starting out the door.

"Wait a minute," she said sharply, grabbing my arm. "What are you going to do? What about Andy?"

"What I'm going to do could get a person in trouble. That's fine for me, but you didn't sign up for hazardous duty."

"Now *that* sounds suspiciously sexist," Annie said, frowning, hands on hips.

"I guess it does at that," I said with a grin. "I retract the statement. And I'll even let you pay your own cab fare home."

"Listen, I am *not* going home until you tell me what this hazardous stuff is all about." Annie was full-fledged angry now, and she planted both booted feet in the hall as if she meant to stay.

"All right, I'll tell you, but only because you're a client of ours, by virtue of being employed by Mills/Lake/Ryman. I am going to pay Mr. Swartz's apartment a visit. Call me the suspicious type, but—"

Annie looked at me incredulously, brushing a hair away from her face with a mittened hand. "That's breaking in," she said, shifting her voice to a loud whisper. "Which is—"

"Which is illegal," I interrupted her back, keeping my own voice low as a couple passed us. "And which is why you should leave. I get paid to do things like this, you don't."

"Stupid things, you mean!" she shout-whispered. "Why do you want to get in there, anyway? Andy'll probably be home soon. I'll bet he got stuck working late at the agency."

"Sure, and he didn't bother to let you know, even though just yesterday he was awfully damn anxious to see you."

Annie's expression had changed from anger to concern. The angry color drained from her cheeks. "Please . . . I'd really like to stay with you," she said, her hand squeezing my forearm.

I took a deep breath and watched the steam from my breath waft over her left shoulder. "Okay, consider yourself an accessory," I told her. "You'll probably get probation when they lock me up. From now on, no talking, got it? And keep your mittens on." She nodded.

The first part came easy—the hall door wasn't even locked; it rubbed against the threshold and didn't close all the way. So much for security in one rehabbed building. The first floor hallway was wallpapered in a blue flowery pattern and the lighting was good—better than I would have liked. We tiptoed past the door of Apartment 1-F, the F apparently for "front," and on down the hall to the rear, where the only other door had to be Swartz's. Sure enough, there was 1-R in brass on it.

It had only one lock, no deadbolt. Apparently the tenants of One-nineteen Charlton were either trusting souls or not very street-smart. The lock looked to be no match for my little pocket kit of tools. Annie watched wide-eyed as I went to work on the cheap Basgall, conquering it in less than forty-five seconds. I put my gloves back on and eased the door open, feeling for a light switch, which I found on the second swipe.

I don't know what registered first, the sound of Annie gasping behind me or the sight of the figure eight feet away on the living-room carpet. He was sprawled with his head on one outstretched arm, and the dark curly hair was matted, as if he'd been out in the rain. His eyes were open. On closer inspection, I could see that the matting had been caused by blood—a lot of it, much of which had soaked into the beige carpet. As I knelt and confirmed that the man on the floor was history, I looked over my shoulder at Annie. She was leaning against the doorframe, her face ashen. The thought crossed my mind that any second, as soon as Swartz's death had time to sink in, she was going to start screaming. Which was the last thing yours truly needed at the moment.

"One, are you okay, and two, is this Swartz?" I demanded. She nodded, numbly.

"He's . . . ?" Her mouth stopped working.

"Believe it," I said quietly, turning back to the late tenant of the apartment and placing my fingertips on his neck to confirm what I'd said, although it was hardly necessary. There was no warmth in the body. The right side of his skull above the forehead was pretty well pushed in, probably by the eight-inch-high abstract metal sculpture on a marble base that was lying on the floor a few feet from him.

"Annie," I said, noting she hadn't taken her gloves off, "you can leave and hope nobody saw you come in. I've got to make some calls—one to the police. Now—"

"I'll stay," she said woodenly.

"Not necessary. I'm used to taking the heat for things like finding my way into domiciles using questionable means, but you're not, and—"

"I said I'll stay!"

I couldn't tell for sure if she was in shock, but I wasn't about to argue with her and rouse the neighbors; they'd know what happened soon enough. I rose and told her to walk out to the front stoop and get some air before coming back in. She nodded, swallowed, and went down the empty hall, looking back uncertainly. I smiled and nodded, attempting an "everything-is-okay" expression, which of course was absurd.

I had damn little time. After she left I gave the body a quick going-over and went to the phone, still wearing gloves myself. The first call was answered on the second ring.

"Me," I said. "I'm in Swartz's apartment. He didn't show in the bar; then we called him and there was no answer, so Annie and I came here, and I sweet-talked the lock. We found him on the floor, as dead as the *Herald-Trib*. Skull dented, lots of blood. Looks like he's been here several hours. Instructions?"

Wolfe took one of his bushel-sized breaths, then cleared his throat. "Have you talked to the police?" His tone was grim.

"Not yet. I thought you might have some sage thoughts at this point."

"*Pfui.* It's too late for sagacity, assuming you would recognize it were it proffered to you. You must of course summon them."

"Believe it or not, that was next on my list of chores. You realize it will mean long hours of questioning and missed meals for yours truly."

"I do," Wolfe said. I swear he almost sounded sympathetic.

EIGHT

Annie hadn't come back yet, so I tried to put what little time I had alone in the apartment to use. The place was nicely furnished in Scandinavian modern, and other than the body and the sculpture, nothing seemed to be out of place. Ditto the bathroom, kitchen, and bedroom, all of which were unusually neat for being a bachelor's quarters.

I knelt and patted down Swartz, who was wearing gray slacks and a blue botton-down oxford-cloth dress shirt, open at the collar. His glasses were in a case in his shirt pocket and his billfold was in the left rear pants pocket. It had the standard identification, including driver's license, three credit cards, and a picture of a couple who probably were his parents, plus seventy-nine dollars in cash and two lottery tickets. The watch on his left wrist was a Rolex—or one of those Asian knockoffs that can fool damn near everybody, me included. But then, I've never been on intimate terms with a Rolex.

The sculpture on the floor appeared to have dried blood on it. The thing was some kind of award—a small gold plaque on the base read AMERICUS SHOW

1987, 1ST PRIZE—SOAPS AND DETERGENTS, ANDREW SWARTZ, COLMAR & CONN. I played Sherlock Holmes and crawled around on the carpet in a four-foot radius of the body, but if there were any clues, they eluded my sub-Sherlockian senses.

Annie walked back in as I was dialing Homicide, my handkerchief wrapped around my hand. I smiled at her and got a sober nod in return; she still looked shaky and didn't hesitate to sit when I motioned her to a white sofa that was well removed from Swartz's corpse.

"You can still leave," I told her. "Otherwise, you'll be having some conversations with the police."

"I don't mind," she said in a strong but wooden voice, keeping her eyes averted from the body.

"Fair enough. Here we go." The receiver at the other end got picked up on the first ring. "Is Sergeant Stebbins there?" I asked the hoarse-voiced detective. It was a long shot given the time of night.

"Purley? Uh—yeah, come to think of it, he still is. Who's calling?"

"Archie Goodwin."

That brought a snort before the guy cupped his receiver and bellowed Purley's name. I've never been terribly popular with the Homicide crowd. For that matter, neither has Wolfe.

"Yeah?"

This was Purley Stebbins's usual salutation. A word here about the good sergeant: He has been employed by the New York Police Department since the days when LaGuardia was a mayor, not an airport, and he has served as Inspector Cramer's right-hand man in Homicide for most of that time. Charm and diplomacy have never been among Purley's high cards, but he got dealt aces in honesty and bravery.

"I'm calling from an apartment in the Village," I told him. "With me is a young woman who was supposed to meet a guy tonight for drinks. The guy, by the name of Andrew Swartz, didn't show, and now we know why: He's lying on the floor here, which is to say his apartment, and he's not taking a nap. And don't waste the taxpayers' money by sending the paramedics; this one's been gone for some time."

Purley muttered something best not repeated, then took a deep breath. "And I suppose you just happened along?" he posed sarcastically.

"It's a complicated story," I answered, giving him the address.

"I'll find time for it," he growled, hanging up harder than was necessary.

"The police will be here within ten minutes," I said to Annie, replacing the receiver and putting the handkerchief back in my pocket. "And we're fortunate in one respect: A sergeant named Stebbins will be talking to you; he's a long way from smooth, but he's a decent man, and he won't waste your time unnecessarily." I could have told her about mopes like Lieutenant Rowcliff and how they handle investigations, but I figured she had enough on her mind right now.

We both walked out to the front stoop and waited for Purley, who didn't make a liar out of me, pulling up eight minutes after he'd banged down the phone. He got out of the front passenger seat of a squad car that was blinking like a pinball machine and plodded up the sidewalk toward us with his uniformed driver three paces behind him. Everything about Purley Stebbins seems to shout cop. He's fairly tall and wide without being fat, with a bony face bracketed by big ears. His overcoat, open despite the thirty-degree weather, revealed a baggy brown suit and a tie of indeterminate color. He gave me one of those are-you-ever-going-to-get-out-of-my-life? looks and uttered a single word: "Where?"

"Rear of this floor," I told him, and Annie and I fell into step behind him and the uniformed cop, whose nameplate read "J. Marshall." We all shouldered our way into the living room, where Purley surveyed the remains of Andrew Swartz for several seconds.

"Howd'ja get in?" he asked me.

"I could tell you that the door was unlocked or ajar, but my mother taught me never to lie."

"Breaking and entering," he muttered, although at the moment he obviously wasn't concerned about that particular breach of the law. "He's where you found him?"

"Hasn't moved a muscle. By the way, this is Annie Burkett, the one Swartz was supposed to meet for drinks."

Purley nodded her way, which for him is the equivalent of a bow, then he knelt next to the body.

"The M.E.'s on the way," he said, turning to me. "I suppose you've given the place a good going over."

"You won't find my fingerprints anywhere, if that's what you're asking. I've had my gloves on except to check Swartz's carotid."

"What time did you get here?" He directed the question at both of us as he slowly got to his feet. I looked at Annie, whose frown made it clear that she expected me to be spokesperson here.

"Just before I phoned you, Purley. Annie had been waiting for Swartz at a bar called Toohey's, which is a five-minute walk from here."

Stebbins grimaced and turned his face into a question mark as he studied us, his eyes moving from me to Annie and back. "You two . . . know each other, right?"

"As of today we do," I said, dodging a lie.

He sucked in almost as much air as Wolfe does and let it out slowly, hitching up his belt. "Tell me why it is that I'm positive there's more to your being here than just random chance?"

"Because you're the suspicious type by nature," I replied. "And I—"

I was interrupted by the sound of a siren. Another car had arrived, and within seconds, Swartz's apartment was overrun. New York's Finest quickly took over. The guy from the medical examiner's office huffed in, along with two more uniforms and a police photographer. Purley eased Annie and me out the door and into the corridor, where tenants of the building were beginning to gather and buzz.

"Miss . . . Burkett, isn't it?" he asked. "We'll need to talk to you. And you too," he said, addressing me in a tone several degrees colder than he used on Annie. "Let's go out to the car."

We elbowed our way through the growing knots of buzzing tenants and out to the car Purley had arrived in. He had us both sit in the back seat and he plumped down up front, turning on the engine and the heater and the dome light and swiveling to face us. "I'd like to start with you," he said to Annie. "This Swartz, was he a good friend of yours?"

"I knew him," she said, clearing her throat, "but not terribly well."

"How did you happen to know him, Miss Burkett?"

She looked questioningly at me, and I gave her a nod, realizing its implications.

"We both work for advertising agencies, and, well . . . he called me, he wanted to talk to me."

"What about?"

She eyed me again and got another nod, which wasn't lost on Purley. What the hell, I thought, it was going to come out soon enough anyway—might as well be right here and now. And that's what happened. Looking at me every thirty seconds for approval, Annie spilled it all: her job at Mills/Lake/Ryman, the apparent commercial idea thefts by Colmar & Conn, the hiring of Wolfe by the agency, Swartz's call to Annie, my trip to the M/L/R office, our rendezvous at Toohey's, and the visit to Swartz's apartment. Purley asked a few questions, but mainly Annie talked, and when she was through, he threw a look my way.

"Got anything to add?"

"Nope. She said it better than I could."

"Uh-huh. What does Wolfe think?"

"Beats me. I've been trying to figure that out for years."

"Don't get cute. You know damn well what I mean—what does he think about this Swartz thing?"

"Hell, Purley, he's not up to date on what's happened."

The dome bulb in the squad car was dim, but it gave off more than enough light to show the cynicism on his face. "I've known you too long," he muttered. "If you didn't call Wolfe before you phoned me, then I'm a parish priest."

"Don't bother going out to buy a collar," I said. "Okay, so I rang Wolfe; after all, I am employed by the man, and I was on a job. But as to what he thinks about Swartz buying the farm, he didn't share it with me. In fact, I don't think he was terribly glad to hear from me."

"I can believe *that.*" Purley said it with feeling. "Okay, I gotta stay here, but I'll have Marshall drive you both to headquarters to make statements."

"Where's Cramer?" I asked.

"Vacation. Gets back tomorrow."

"Does that mean we draw Rowcliff?"

Purley came as close to smiling as he ever does, then shook his head. "Sorry, he's off today. You'll probably get Phelps—a real softie."

In fact, Lieutenant Phelps of Homicide, whom I had never met before, was hardly a softie. When we got to headquarters, Annie and I were of course split up. I assumed that Phelps talked to her first, because I sat in a gray room alone for two hours, counting the places on the ceiling where the paint had peeled. I was up to ninety-two when Phelps breezed in.

"So . . . you're Archie Goodwin," he said, rubbing his hands together and grinning tightly. He was tall and thin, with blond hair beginning to go white. Somebody most have told him once that he was good-looking, because he had that pleased-with-himself look usually worn on the faces of second-rate film actors. "I know all about you. The word around is you think you're quite the smart guy."

I looked up at Phelps, expressionless. "You must have me confused with someone else."

"I don't think so," he said, still holding the Jack Palance smile and squinting with his light blue eyes as he sat on the corner of the table in the typical cop-in-the-movie pose. "I've heard a lot about you from Lieutenant Rowcliff, who you know."

"That name sounds vaguely familiar."

"Listen Goodwin, Stebbins radioed ahead, so I know all about tonight. Plus the nice little chat I just had with Miss Burkett. You're already in the soup on illegal entry, so don't make it any worse on yourself. Now exactly what were you doing at Swartz's place?"

"If you talked to Purley and had such a pleasant powwow with Miss Burkett, you already have the answer to that," I told him.

"I'd like to hear it from you, though—and I've got all night." Maybe his facial muscles were frozen into that sneer.

"Fine, then let's get someone in here to take it down," I said in an exasperated tone, "because I'm only going to tell it once."

"I'll decide just how many times you tell it, mister," Phelps hissed, but he did get a young uniformed cop in to take shorthand.

The next forty minutes are best summarized. First off, Phelps possesses all the makings of Homicide's next Rowcliff—he's arrogant, oafish, stupid, and rude, although I haven't seen enough of him to know what his weaknesses are. His neo-Spanish-Inquisition interrogation style wears a little thin after the first twenty seconds or so, but I thought I was the model of patience as I calmly recited the events of the evening, and also confirmed what he already knew: that M/L/R was a client of Nero Wolfe. At various times during the questioning, he threatened to (a) lock me up, (b) get Wolfe downtown immediately, and (c) revoke my private investigator's license. I could have played games with him to see if, like Rowcliff, he stutters when he gets angry. But he wasn't worth the effort, and besides, I was tired and hungry, so I rode out his tantrums and his posturing.

"All right, Goodwin," he said after he'd exhausted his questions and threats, "that's it for now. You can clear out. But you'd better believe you haven't heard the last of me."

I almost drew blood on my lower lip stopping myself from responding to that, but as much as I would have liked to tweak Phelps, I was more interested in getting home. As it was, for some reason I had a devil of a time finding a cab, and when I finally rang the bell on the stoop of the brownstone for Fritz to unbolt the door, it was almost one. Wolfe had gone up to bed, and there were no notes on my desk. Knowing that tomorrow—make that today—was likely to be hectic, I shut off the phone and climbed the stairs to my room. I'm used to eight hours of sleep, but I was ready to settle for six.

NINE

I've talked—make that griped—on more than a few occasions about Wolfe's inflexibility when it comes to the daily schedule in the brownstone. However, in the interest of fairness, I must report that I've got an inflexibility of my own: breakfast. Barring nuclear alert or tidal wave, I take my morning meal at a small table in the kitchen Monday through Saturday. It consists of some combination of coffee, juice, muffins, wheatcakes, eggs, and a breakfast meat, chewed and/or swallowed leisurely and seasoned with healthy dollops of the *New York Times*.

Fritz knows that during this period, I accept no calls, except from Wolfe, who has his own breakfast on a tray in his bedroom, and who has been known to ask for me at this time about as frequently as a total solar eclipse. Wednesday morning while gnawing on sausage and the *Times*, I could tell that Fritz was dying to break in, but I wasn't about to give him the opening—not yet, anyway. Fritz, as you may know, frets when Wolfe isn't working on a case and thereby earning a fat fee, because he thinks we're always three days removed from bankruptcy court. I hadn't told him yet about

Mills/Lake/Ryman hiring us, and I doubt if Wolfe had filled him in, either. But it was obvious from the way he hovered over me that he had what he felt was exciting news.

I ate at my usual speed, however, lingering over a *Times* analysis of the Mets' chances ("anywhere from first to fifth") for the coming season. The paper had no mention of young Swartz's death—they undoubtedly learned about it too late to make the home-delivered edition. Finally, after draining the last coffee from the cup, I wiped my mouth with the napkin and turned to Fritz. "Any calls?" I asked innocently.

"Archie, they started right at six, when I turned the telephone on!" he blurted. "Already, seven people have called, all for you. They are about . . . something that happened last night." He made that last sentence sound like a question.

"Something *did* happen last night—to a man named Swartz," I told him, neatly refolding my *Times*. "And in reply to your unasked query, it may or may not result in more business for us. By the way, Mr. Wolfe has a new client, an advertising agency, and it is entirely possible that Mr. Swartz's murder may somehow be tied to what we've just started working on. Who called?"

"First the *Times*, at six-oh-three," Fritz said, reading off the little pad he keeps next to the kitchen telephone. "A reporter named Lopossa, who said that he'd been trying our line for over an hour. Then Channel Two, at six-nineteen, Mr. Cohen seven minutes later, then a Mr. Mills, then the *Daily News* at—"

"Enough," I said, holding up a hand. "Give me your notes, and I'll start returning these—after I talk to Mr.

Wolfe." Fritz didn't say a word, but as he turned back to his kitchen chores, I detected a slight off-key humming.

Wolfe's bedroom is on the second floor of the brownstone, directly beneath mine. I took the stairs two at a time and knocked on his door, getting a gruff "Yes?"

"Me. We need to talk." The second yes was gruffer than the first, but without the question mark, so I entered. As many times as I've seen Wolfe having breakfast in bed, the sight still awes me: Dressed as usual in his bright yellow pajamas and propped up with the tray on his lap, he seems somehow larger than when he's behind his desk. Maybe it's because of all that yellow—the coverlet is almost the same color as the pajamas—but he is indeed a sight to behold, and one that only Fritz and I are ever likely to see.

"Well?" he said, glowering at me between bites of eggs *au beurre noir.*

"I know that you'd prefer my giving you a recap of last night after your visit to the orchids, but this is an exception, partly because first thing this morning we got a slug of phone calls about Swartz—Fritz took them all—and I need some marching orders before returning them."

Without waiting for a response, I launched into a report on what had happened after I phoned Wolfe from Swartz's apartment, closing with an observation that the police were probably more than glad to mention my name often in their report, knowing it would sic the newspaper and TV folks on us. He stopped eating during my recitation, pausing only to drink chocolate. After I finished, he sighed as only he can sigh. "One of those calls was of course Mr. Mills," he said sourly.

"As a matter of fact, you are correct. All the rest are from the media."

"Get him," Wolfe snapped, moving his head a sixteenth of an inch in the direction of the telephone on his nightstand. Heaven forbid he should have to push the buttons himself.

I punched up the number, which apparently was Mills's home, and he answered on the first ring. "Mr. Mills, Archie Goodwin returning your call. Nero Wolfe wants to speak to you." I handed the receiver to Wolfe and stood back. I'm used to listening in on his calls at my desk in the office, and it's hard hearing only half a conversation; although in this case, it was simple to figure out what was being said on the other end, especially because Wolfe, bless him, was kind enough to repeat or rephrase much of Mills's talk, presumably for my benefit.

"Yes, sir, Mr. Goodwin has apprised me of last night's events. Yes, I agree that this complicates matters. Yes, I can appreciate that Miss Burkett is shaken and depressed . . . No, sir, it is not unusual for the police to question the first person to arrive at a murder scene for over an hour—sometimes rather forcefully . . ."

Wolfe then listened for close to a minute, his scowl growing by degrees. When Mills finally wound down, he sighed. "I understand your concern, but since Miss Burkett has shared with the police the reason for our having been hired, it becomes fair game for the press, who no doubt will eagerly pursue this facet. Be prepared for them when you reach your office. Indeed, we already have received numerous calls from the newspapers and television stations, none of which has yet been returned. And as you are undoubtedly aware, Mr. Goodwin and I are popular targets of these people . . . Yes, I agree that you can terminate our agreement if you so choose, although we already have deposited your check for twenty-five thousand dollars, which is nonrefundable."

Wolfe was silent again for the better part of a minute, still scowling. He never likes talking on the phone, and it becomes intolerable when this activity interrupts a meal—even breakfast. Finally he cut in on Mills. "Of course this all is extremely uncomfortable for you and your colleagues, especially as the press will surely report that your security has been breached by a rival agency. But think of the discomfort Mr. Swartz endured."

That must have gotten to Mills, because he said something that Wolfe later told me bordered on an apology for being so flinty. Wolfe closed the conversation by telling him that I would call him later in the morning. So we still had a client.

"I appreciate your parroting Mills's half of that little chat," I said. "Sorry to have interrupted your breakfast, but I needed—still do—instructions."

That drew a look that told me that Wolfe indeed wanted to finish his breakfast—alone. But he knew he had to get rid of me first. "Archie, kindly respond to those other callers. I assume Mr. Cohen was among them?"

"You assume correctly."

"Call him first, and be generous with him regarding specifics—within reason, of course. The others can be dealt with in a more perfunctory manner."

"Precisely what I had planned to do," I said, bowing and backing out the door, closing it after me.

When I settled in back at my desk in the office, I tapped out Lon's number. He answered halfway through the first ring.

"Goodwin, reporting as requested, your eminence."

"Archie, for God's sake, what's going on with this Swartz thing? I mean, you call me two days ago asking advertising questions, and then some young advertising whiz gets offed in his Village digs. And damned if we don't learn from the police report that you're the one who finds the body, while in the company of a young woman. And then we hear, never mind how, that you and Wolfe are involved in trying to prove this guy Swartz's agency is stealing ideas from another Madison Avenue bunch—your clients, no less, the very folks you questioned me about."

"Amazingly small world, isn't it? By the way, they're not on Madison Avenue—our clients, that is. Never have been. Let's get our facts straight, soldier."

"All right, dammit, I'm speaking figuratively, and you know it. Stop evading the issue. Now what's the story?"

I gave Lon the story, at least a fair chunk of it, including a description of Swartz's living room when we found him. Lon, first and foremost a thorough reporter, regardless of his position at the *Gazette,* continued peppering me with questions. I answered several of them, ducked a few, and finally called a cease-fire. "Enough—you've got all I can give you, which is more than anybody else is going to receive from this precinct—and that includes Lopossa at the *Times*."

"Why should anybody else get *anything*?" he barked. "After all I've done for you through the years."

"We've done a thing or two for you along the way, too, as in a scrapbook full of scoops. And after all, it's simply smart business for us to stay on good terms with all our friends in the Fourth Estate."

"You and Wolfe are publicity hounds," he muttered, hanging up. I know Lon well enough to realize he was almost half-kidding. I then called the other papers and TV stations, giving them brief recitations of last night's events. They all wanted more, particularly the very persistent woman from the *Daily News*. And one station said they were sending a camera crew right over, but I told them the door would be barred to them, and that we had a Doberman we can't afford to adequately feed. One of Wolfe's many rules is that no TV camera crew is ever to be admitted to the brownstone, that dictum dating from when a local station referred to him as "an eccentric and obese recluse," although in truth, Wolfe's abhorrence of television news coverage predated that event by many years.

It took me more than an hour to return the calls and deal with three new ones, two from radio stations and the other from a suburban paper over in Jersey. I finally finished, stretched, and went to the kitchen for a coffee refill, asking Fritz to answer the telephone and take messages until further notice. I was talked out and tired of answering questions, many of them stupid. I carried the coffee back to my desk, riffled through the mail, none of which was interesting, and stacked it on Wolfe's desk blotter.

Next, I started tackling a major housecleaning of our files. I had tried to persuade Wolfe to switch to a computerized filing system, showing him how much space we could save by using disks, but he wasn't having any; for him, correspondence will always mean paper, nothing else. However, I did get him to agree to get rid of letters more than ten years old, the bulk of them correspondence with orchid growers around the country and the world. I had manila folders spread out all over my desktop when I heard the whirr of the elevator and checked my watch. Sure enough, it had somehow gotten to be eleven o'clock, and his largeness was descending from his morning orchid therapy.

Because we already had conversed, Wolfe dispensed with his usual inquiry as to how I'd slept, and, after placing a raceme of *Laelia Milleri* in his desk vase, began attacking the mail. He'd been at it all of two minutes when the front doorbell rang.

"Want to make bets on who that is?" I asked, cocking an eyebrow.

"There can be no wager, as we would choose the same individual," he replied peevishly.

"Assuming it's who we think it is, should I let him in?"

Wolfe dipped his head a fraction of an inch, his version of a nod, and turned back to the mail. I went to the front hall and peered through the one-way panel in the door, confirming what we both already knew.

"Inspector, how nice to see you," I said with what I felt was convincing heartiness as I swung the door open. "Been on vacation?"

"Ice fishing, Upstate," growled L. T. Cramer, head of Homicide for the New York Police Department, as he stormed into the hall. "Wolfe down from the plant rooms?"

I said yes, but he was already barreling toward the office at full speed, which is impressive for a man his size. By the time I reached the office door, Cramer was thudding into the red leather chair. Wolfe considered him without enthusiasm.

"Four lousy days I'm away from the job," Cramer rasped, jabbing an unlit cigar in Wolfe's direction, "and what happens? A well-known young adman gets himself killed at home in the Village—just the kind of story the press goes nuts over—and who finds the body but your jack-of-all-troubles here." He flipped a scowl my way and turned back to Wolfe as if daring contradiction.

"I too was surprised," Wolfe said mildly. "Will you have something to drink?"

"I didn't come to socialize!" Cramer bellowed, leaning forward in the chair and jabbing with the cigar some more. "I want to know precisely why Goodwin was in Swartz's apartment in the first place, never mind for the moment that he picked the lock."

Wolfe raised his eyebrows. "Mr. Goodwin left me with the distinct impression that he was most candid with your associate last night. Archie?"

"I gave Phelps the whole thing," I told Cramer. "By the way, he's a little smoother than Rowcliff, but not much."

Cramer used a word that indicated he wasn't impressed with Phelps, either. "Okay, I know you told him all about you and Wolfe having that Mills agency as a client, along with the reason they hired you—big deal. Hell, you weren't doing us any favors. You'd already heard the Burkett woman telling Purley the same thing when the three of you were sitting in the squad car. We can thank her for your so-called candor."

"That's taking a pretty cynical attitude," I said.

"And speaking of Annie Burkett," Cramer snapped, ignoring my remark, "how well do you know her?"

"I just met her yesterday, like I told Phelps."

"How much do you know *about* her?"

"Other than the few observations that I formed during the short time we were together, only what the partners at M/L/R said about her—which is basically that she's one hell of an art director. Sara Ryman is particularly high on her."

"Uh-huh. What about her social life?" Cramer asked.

"Believe it or not, I can't help you there—maybe that shows that I'm slipping."

"Maybe. Any idea how well she knew Swartz?"

"That much I *do* know—at least from her lips. I asked her about him yesterday morning, right after we met in the agency's offices, and she told me about his call to her. She said a friend of hers had gone out with him, which is how they met."

"But the two of them never went out together?"

"So she said."

Cramer chewed on his cigar, his eyes moving from me to Wolfe and back again. "You say you may be slipping, but I don't believe it, not when it comes to reading women. Do you believe her?"

I shrugged. "Thanks for the vote of confidence. At this point, I'd have to say yes. She a suspect?"

"At this point, why not?"

"No reason, other than what's the motive? Any chance this was a gay murder?" I asked.

"Everything's possible, of course," Cramer grumbled, "but I'd give long odds on that. We've talked to a couple of Swartz's drinking buddies—two guys who live in the neighborhood—and they tell us he was quite the ladies' man. His address book seems to bear that out, too. There were a dozen women's names in it—including Miss Burkett's, by the way. But then, maybe you already know that."

"If you're not-so-subtly suggesting that I peeked into his little black book, try again."

"Then maybe you *are* slipping. Whose idea was it to go to Swartz's apartment when he didn't show up in the bar—yours or Miss Burkett's?"

"Mine. She wasn't overly enthusiastic about it."

"But once inside, you gave the place a thorough going-over, right?" He doesn't give up easily.

"Mr. Cramer," Wolfe cut in, "we have indulged you generously. Archie has patiently answered your questions, many of which had been put to him by your associate Mr. Phelps."

"Look, I'm doing some indulging of my own," Cramer shot back, the color rising in his face. "I'm willing to look the other way on the breaking-and-entering business, but I'd like a little consideration myself."

"And you are getting it," Wolfe said. "That does not, however, extend to impugning Archie's veracity."

"Well, excuse me!" Cramer huffed, proving once again that he'll never make it as a stand-in for Steve Martin. "I didn't realize we'd gotten so thin-skinned these days."

"Come now, sir," Wolfe said, showing admirable

restraint. "This outrage does not become you. You cannot deny that we have been cooperative."

"Compared to what? I don't know anything that I didn't know when I walked in the front door."

"That is because of Archie's candor during his interrogation last night."

"Candor, my foot!" Cramer barked, standing up and flinging his cigar at the wastebasket, missing it by a yard. "There's more here than I'm getting, and we all know it. All right, dammit, I'm leaving, but by God, if either of you step off the path on this one—and for all I know you already have—you'll find your licenses gone faster than you can say Cuomo." He did one of his snappier about-faces and left at the same speed he came in, again with me trailing in his wake.

TEN

"Well, there's one for Ripley's column," I said when I got back to the office after bolting the door behind Cramer, who had climbed into an unmarked car that was idling at the curb. "He gets the truth, and he doesn't believe it."

Wolfe took a healthy swig of the beer that Fritz had brought in during the Inspector's tirade. "He's flailing about, as he so often does, and we are a convenient target of his vituperation."

"All of that," I said, nodding and making a mental note to look up vituperation when Wolfe wasn't around, although I was pretty sure of its meaning. "What now? Do you want me to call Mills, as you had promised I would?"

"Yes."

"Any instructions as to what I tell him?"

Wolfe picked up his book and stroked the cover. "You did not talk to all the people you had hoped to when you were there yesterday. Another visit is called for."

"Agreed. You want to listen in?"

Wolfe nodded and after I got the number, he picked up his receiver. I had no trouble getting through to Mills.

"Goodwin—this place is a madhouse," he blurted. "We've had newspaper reporters and TV crews and police tramping all over the place. Nobody can get a damn thing done. And that's only the half of—"

"How's Annie?" I interrupted.

"A basket case, of course. I called her at home before I got to work and told her not to come in today, and to take her phone off the hook. Hell, she's the one most of the press that showed up here wanted to talk to. Although they're all hot to know more about the cherry drink stuff, too. So are the police; a guy named Phelps has been getting in everybody's hair all morning. That's bad enough, but then Foreman called in, and he's really livid."

"About the publicity?"

"That's part of it, but he's also teed off because nobody here bothered to tell him about our hiring Wolfe. He wants to know why he wasn't brought in on the decision. I took the rap for that with him."

"But he's still angry?"

"Hah, you'd better believe it. In fact, I was about to call you, to warn you that Foreman's going to be phoning Wolfe."

"We can hardly wait. Say, when I was at the agency yesterday, I wasn't able to see Lake. I thought I might stop by this afternoon and—"

"I'd really prefer it if you wait," Mills said pleadingly. "We're so up for grabs today that everybody needs a little time to catch their breath. How about tomorrow?" I looked at Wolfe, who nodded, and said tomorrow would be fine, first thing in the morning.

"So, now what?" I asked Wolfe after hanging up.

He had just opened his book, and set it down, looking irritated. "It appears that we will be hearing from Mr. Foreman. I suggest that you gather information on the gentleman." That was Wolfe's way of getting rid of me, at least until lunch.

I pulled down the *Who's Who* from the bookshelf and found to my surprise that Acker Foreman had no listing. The guy apparently really was a recluse, as Mills had said. Next I went to the shelf where we keep the most recent month's copies of the *Times* and *Gazette*; Wolfe wasn't the only one who remembered seeing Foreman's picture last week in the *Gazette*. The photo, of Acker and Arnold, was in the first section, and the caption said they were leaving court after testifying in a trademark case that was decided in Cherr-o-key's favor. There was no accompanying story. I clipped out the photo, put it on Wolfe's desk blotter, then I turned on my phone and called Lon Cohen for the second time that day.

"So, you've decided to spill the whole thing, eh?" he said when he heard my voice. "Good thinking."

"Nothing to spill—at least not yet. And when there is, you'll get it as usual. I need some information."

"Why do I feel I'm being used?"

"Hell, nobody's ever gotten the best of you in your life. Now cut out the martyr bit and tell me everything you know about Acker Foreman."

"Ah, of course. As in Cherr-o-key, whose agency—your client—has had its commercial ideas pilfered by the guys who do ads for AmeriCherry, one of whom is suddenly very dead."

"You're a quick study—I've always said it. Now what about Foreman?"

"Strange bird," Lon replied, his tone suddenly businesslike. "At one time, he was pretty flamboyant—he was an inventor, still holds a batch of patents, mainly in plastics if I remember right. He also had something to do with developing the automatic transmission for cars way back when. And he also started an airline, which he sold, making acres of money in the process. His worth is supposed to be in the billions—hell, one of the business magazines ranked him one of the five wealthiest Americans last year, if I remember right. But the last few years, he's pulled the hermit bit like Howard Hughes and gotten secretive about himself. Hell, he's hardly ever photographed anymore, and he refuses all requests for interviews. We tried to send a reporter over to his offices on Sixth Avenue to do a profile on him when he turned seventy-five a couple of years ago, and his bodyguards got nasty, which was Foreman's way of telling us to get lost. He wouldn't talk to anybody in the media, for that matter. Hasn't for ages."

"Although you had that picture of him and one of his sons in the paper last week?"

"Yeah, but only because they had to show up in court on that case involving their name. It was a stupid suit to begin with—the plaintiff didn't have a case. That's why we only gave it a photo. Our reporter tried to talk to Foreman—so did everybody else, for that matter, but he and the son just walked out of court and got into a limo without saying a damn word."

"So he lives in New York?"

"At least occasionally. He's got an apartment on the East Side—Sutton or Beekman, I forget which. But he spends a lot more of his time at a big estate down south of Washington, and he's also got a ranch about the size of Delaware out in Oklahoma, which is where he comes from. Apparently he still flies his own jet around."

"Family?"

"About two years ago, he split from wife number three, who's at least twenty years younger than he is, maybe more. First two marriages also ended in divorce. He's got a pair of sons from spouse number two—they're around forty, both divorced themselves, and work for the old man at Cherr-o-key, which is privately owned, as in Acker Foreman has practically all the stock. Word is that the boys aren't overly cerebral, but that Dad insists on having them around. Among long-time Cherr-o-key employees, they're something of a not-so-funny joke."

"How did Foreman get into the soft drink business in the first place?"

"Among his other talents, the guy's quite a chemist, and back in the sixties, or so the Cherr-o-key gospel reads, he developed a 'new' formula for a cherry-flavored, noncaffeinated drink. For years it didn't do very well, but now that the country has tilted away from caffeine, his drink is hot stuff."

"You seem to be up on Mr. Foreman."

"I should be. At the daily doping session this morning, our advertising columnist talked a lot about him. Because of what's happened with Cherr-o-key and AmeriCherry, we're planning a big feature for Sunday on ad agencies swiping ideas from each other."

That ought to make Mills's day. "Anybody at your place talked to Foreman?"

"No, but we're sure as hell trying. We can't even find out if he's in town. I might ask you the same question."

"Haven't the foggiest," I said, mentally crossing my fingers. "I do know, through the folks at M/L/R, that he's not very happy."

"Yeah, our ad columnist talked to Mills, and he was able to worm that much out of him, if nothing else. Listen, Archie, I'm counting on you to come through for us."

"Have you talked to the people at Colmar and Conn?" I asked, ducking his plea.

"Dammit, they're as closed-mouthed as Mills, although they've got good reason to be. They don't want to talk about idea-thievery."

"But now with what's happened to Swartz, they may have to, at least to the police," I said. "What about Harlowe Conn?"

"What about him?" Lon sounded exasperated. "God, you've sure got enough questions—but no answers, at least not for an old friend. I've talked enough, and we've got deadlines. Call me back when you're prepared to be the talker." He hung up before I could get in the last word. That made it twice in one day.

"Well, I got some information on the eremitic Mr. Foreman," I said to the cover of Wolfe's book, thinking my use of a fifteen-dollar word would get his attention. I was wrong, and I turned back to the file folders on my desk, but before I could even open one, the phone rang.

"Mr. Acker Foreman calling Nero Wolfe," a crisp

female voice intoned. I asked her to please wait and covered my mouthpiece. "It's Foreman," I told Wolfe, who this time lowered the book and reached for his instrument.

"This is Nero Wolfe," he said as I stayed on the line.

"A moment please for Mr. Foreman," Ms. Crisp Voice said. She hit the hold button, and Wolfe looked like he was going to hang up. Nobody enjoys that "you-get-on-the-phone-first" stunt, Wolfe least of all. But he didn't have to wait more than a handful of seconds.

"Nero Wolfe?" a gravelly voice burst loudly onto the line, not waiting for an answer to his question. "This is Acker Foreman. I need to see you. Today."

"Indeed?" Wolfe replied coolly.

"You know why," Foreman shot back. He wasn't exactly oozing social graces.

"Perhaps you can enlighten me," Wolfe replied, still as cool as a fall evening in the Vermont mountains.

"Let's not waste time sparring. I read the papers. I know you're bright—some say you're a sort of genius, but that's been said about me, too. Words like 'genius' are overused and therefore devalued, particularly the way the press throws them around. Can you be here in an hour? My office is on Sixth Avenue, the address is—"

"I will not be there in an hour, or ever," Wolfe said evenly. "I make it a practice to avoid leaving home save in exceptional circumstances."

"This is an exceptional circumstance."

"For you, perhaps; for me, no. If you wish to see me, sir, it will be here, providing that we can agree upon a time."

That slowed Foreman down, as it was meant to. "Don't try to get tough with me, or you'll regret it," he rasped after several ticks of the clock.

Wolfe neatly aligned his book with the edge of his desk before responding. "My stance is not meant to be tough, merely firm," he replied. "In this instance, you are the petitioner. Were our roles reversed, I would doubtless be compelled to venture forth to Sixth Avenue. Manifestly, that is not the case."

"Give your address to my secretary," Foreman snapped. "I will be there at two."

"I will not be available at two," Wolfe parried. "Three o'clock is acceptable, however, and my associate, Mr. Goodwin, will supply the address to you—but to no one else. Please hold on."

Wolfe gently cradled the receiver, returning to his book. "Mr. Foreman, this is Archie Goodwin," I said politely, proceeding to give him the address. I assumed he was taking it down, although I heard nothing other than a sniff on the other end until, after several seconds, there was a click, and the dial tone began droning.

"Not a terribly sociable fellow, is he?" I said, but Wolfe was buried in his book again, where he would stay until we went into the dining room to tackle Fritz's chicken livers and tomatoes, followed by rice cakes.

ELEVEN

Wolfe had read an essay someplace to the effect that baseball more than any other single pastime or activity encapsulates the composite American character, whatever that means. Anyway, during lunch, he asked me a pile of questions about what baseball means to me, being as how I've spent so many hours at Shea Stadium through the years.

I should mention here that although he once went to a World Series game—by way of indulging a foreign guest—Wolfe's knowledge of baseball is probably comparable to my intimacy with the writings of Montaigne. But he was serious—he really wanted to know what it is about the sport that captivates me and millions of our fellow countrymen. And since he refuses to discuss business in the dining room, I was only too glad to expound on a subject I know more about than he does.

"Well," I said between bites of chicken liver, "for instance, when Dwight Gooden is pitching for the Mets, it's as if I'm out there on the mound myself. I like to imagine that I can feel the pressure he's feeling, what with forty-odd thousand people all willing him to strike out the batter."

"But would you really like to *be* Mr. Gooden?" he asked.

"Absolutely not. It's one thing to imagine the pressure, quite another to *live* it, or so I can guess. That kind of pressure I can live without. I'll take a box seat, thanks, along with a hot dog, a scorecard, and enough voice to tell the umpire what I think of him every couple of innings."

That set Wolfe to musing over whether the majority of baseball fans—or "aficionados" as he insists on calling them—have any interest in the technical aspects of the game, or are experiencing it only on a visceral level.

"If I understand what 'visceral' means, and I've got a pretty good idea, then with me it's some of both," I told him. "But for most of the mob at your average game, it's strictly us-versus-them and to the devil with intricacies and strategies."

Our baseball discussion went on through the end of the meal, and then it was back to the office for coffee. At my request, Fritz had gone out for an early copy of the *Gazette*, which was on my desk. Our home-delivered edition doesn't come until after four, and I didn't want to wait that long.

Swartz's murder was played in the lower left-hand corner of page one, under a two-column headline that read ADMAN FOUND SLAIN IN VILLAGE FLAT. The piece was a straightforward recitation. Time of death, according to the police, was between four and six P.M. Mention was made that Annie and I had been the ones who found the body, and there were a few lines on how Wolfe had been hired by Mills/Lake/Ryman to look into what the article called "idea espionage" involving the highly lucrative cherry drink campaigns.

Harlowe Conn was quoted as saying Swartz had been "one of the finest creative talents in advertising history, a tragic loss." But he refused comment on any possible connection between his death and his work on the AmeriCherry campaign. Likewise, Rod Mills had no comment on the competitive battle.

"Here it is," I told Wolfe, laying the paper in front of him. "The good news, they spelled both our names right; the bad news—no pictures."

The truth is, Wolfe enjoys seeing his picture in the paper as much as the next person, maybe more, but he ignored my comment as he digested the article. I then gave him a fill-in on what Lon had told me about Foreman, but he seemed more interested in his latest book, *Adlai Stevenson: His Life and Legacy*, by Porter McKeever, which he plunged into while I was still talking about our next visitor.

As it turned out, Acker Foreman had at least one thing going in his favor: promptness. The doorbell rang precisely at three. I went to the hall and through the one-way glass got an eyeful of a trio. Foreman was in the middle. He was my height, give or take an inch, with a long, narrow, slightly ruddy face and a sparse crop of white hair, which was combed straight back. His eyes were dark—almost black—and they darted nervously from under bushy white brows.

He was flanked by young men, at least young by comparison to him, and neither of them qualified as a bodyguard. It wasn't only that they were skinny and slope-shouldered, but they seemed limp, although admittedly that was a snap judgment based on a five-second gander through the glass. The one on his left I recognized from the *Gazette* photo as Arnold. I walked back to the office.

"Our guest has arrived with two pals," I told Wolfe. "One is son Arnold, and were I the wagering sort, I'd say the other was son Stephen. You remember—the pair Mills said were a pain you-know-where and that Lon referred to as a 'not so funny joke' around the soft drink offices. Do I let them in with the old man? Wait—before you answer, you should know that I can handle both of them if they decide to get cute." Wolfe pursed his lips and nodded, taking a long swallow of beer. He's never been one to start working without fortification.

By this time, the bell was ringing again—a series of short, angry squawks. I went back down the hall and swung open the front door. "You would be Mr. Foreman, I presume?" I asked cheerfully.

"Took you long enough to get here," Foreman snapped, stepping into the hall and motioning his escorts in with a toss of the head. "You Goodwin?"

I said I was and quickly slammed the front door, leaving the two bozos out in the cold.

"What the hell are you doing?" Foreman spat hoarsely, raising a hand as if to karate-chop me. "Those are my sons."

"Sorry for that, but you should have told us on the phone that they were going to be tagging along. We don't like surprises," I told him as the boys began banging on the front door and yelling.

I reopened the door and they burst into the hall. "You okay, Dad?" the one with the dark-rimmed glasses blustered, panting.

"Yes, dammit, I'm fine. Goodwin, this is Stephen"—he gestured curtly toward the blusterer—"and Arnold." They could have been anywhere from the mid-thirties to the mid-forties, each of them a couple inches shorter than their old man, each with unruly black hair, and each shortchanged in the chin department, to say nothing of their manners.

I helped Foreman off with his cashmere overcoat and let Steve and Arnie wrestle with their own. My butler's license covers only invited guests.

"Just a second, Champ," I said to Arnie, moving quickly and twisting his left arm behind him. I reached inside his suitcoat and found what I was looking for, relieving him of it in a smooth motion. "That's two surprises," I said to Foreman Senior, palming a thirty-two-caliber automatic. "One more and you're out."

"Arnold, I told you that kind of thing wasn't necessary!" the billionaire snarled, giving his son a laser-beam look.

"But, Dad, you can't be sure that—"

"Shut up!" Foreman said, turning my way. "They think I can't handle myself, but I've been doing nicely since before they—and you—were born."

"I don't doubt it," I told him. "And if Arnie here insists on wearing a shoulder holster, be sure he tells his tailor to make the proper alterations when he gets fitted for his next suit. He walked in here with a protrusion the size of a small Alp. Now you—take your suitcoat off," I told Stephen, the one wearing glasses.

"I'm not carrying a gun," he protested, hunching his shoulders. "I've never even fired one."

"That's easy to believe, but off with the coat, or no one, and that includes Dad, goes one step farther."

Steve was in a bind, but his father ended the dilemma. "Take off your coat," he said quietly. Like Wolfe, Foreman could get the maximum impact without raising his voice. The red-faced son peeled off his brown plaid sportcoat and handed it to me.

I patted it down and gave it back. "Okay," I told him, "I realize you weren't bulging at the seams like your sibling, but after his little stunt, I was afraid you might have a Derringer tucked away." I patted down Steve's trouser pockets for good measure and led the Foreman crew to the office. As I got to the door, Wolfe set his book down and looked a question at me.

"A little discussion over firearms," I answered, displaying the thirty-two. "It got settled, though, and I'm holding this in trust until adjournment. This is Acker Foreman and his offspring, Stephen and pistol-packin' Arnold." Wolfe favored the old man with one of his millimetric nods, ignoring the boys.

"Lord, I heard you were heavy, but I had no idea," Foreman said, settling into the red leather chair while Curly and Moe plopped into the yellow ones. "Man, don't you know what that does to your system? I weigh exactly what I did sixty years ago, and the reason is, I watch what I eat—and what I don't eat. And I mean every day. I haven't tasted meat since the fifties, and—"

"Sir, I wasn't of the impression you sought this meeting to discuss my well-being," Wolfe said. "Would you like anything to drink? As you see, I'm having beer."

"I don't touch alcohol, and neither do these two," Foreman replied curtly.

"We've got coffee and tea," I offered.

"No thank you," Foreman said, squaring his shoulders. "Caffeine's out, too." The guy may have been in his late seventies, but he cut a lean, healthy figure, and his pricey navy blue pinstripe suit didn't hurt that image any. "Wolfe here is right—we didn't come to talk about his dietary habits, although Lord knows, he could use counseling. But that's his affair. What I'm here to find out"—he turned from me to Wolfe—"is why you're involved in this business with my advertising agency?"

Wolfe looked at him without enthusiasm. "I have a client, sir, and I consider the relationship to be privileged."

"Come now, that high-sounding stuff is fine when you're being grilled by some churlish newspaper reporter, but we're talking informally here," Foreman said in what for him probably was a friendly tone.

"Indeed?" Wolfe raised his eyebrows and came forward in his chair, placing both hands palm down on the desktop. "I'm not in the habit of indulging in badinage upon a first meeting."

"I didn't have you pegged as quite so arrogant," Foreman fired back as both of his sons smirked and Arnie let loose with a guffaw. I was beginning to enjoy the proceedings. "Blazes, it's not as if you don't know who I am," he continued.

"Actually, I know very little about you," Wolfe countered. "You seem to pride yourself on being secretive and reclusive, which in and of itself is not unadmirable, as long as the quest for privacy stops short of obsession."

"And you're suggesting that I'm obsessive?"

"I don't have adequate information on which to

base such a suggestion. And in candor, I have not delved into your vitae. I am, of course, aware of certain things that are public knowledge—among them that in the forties your former partner in an Oklahoma trucking company sued you for mismanagement of funds and that you settled out of court for about a half-million dollars."

"Four hundred thousand and change," Foreman muttered. His sons had stopped smirking.

"Just so. Also, after you sold your airline, the purchaser, a major national carrier, discovered that a number of your planes had serious mechanical deficiencies, and they entered into litigation to reclaim a portion of the purchase price."

"I was *not* aware of those problems when I sold out," Foreman answered, his voice rising.

"I am not suggesting you were. I merely wished to display the admittedly meager scope of my knowledge about you."

"So noted," the billionaire said sourly, making an effort to remain calm, although it was obvious Wolfe had gotten his goat. "Now, about Mills and his ad agency, you're aware that I'm by far their largest client?" Wolfe nodded.

"That being the case, I have every right to know what's going on between you and them."

"Then ask Mr. Mills or one of his partners," Wolfe said. "They, of all people, are beholden to you."

"Dad, this isn't accomplishing a damn thing. Let's get the hell out of here," Arnie squawked, getting up.

"Sit down!" If a voice can sound like a rifle shot, Foreman's did, and Arnie promptly deflated back into the chair. "Wolfe, I *have* talked to Rod Mills, and he says he hired you because neither he nor any of his people were getting to first base in trying to find the leak of ideas over to that foul agency of AmeriCherry's. Of course he didn't bother to tell me that he came to you—I had to read about it in the goddamn papers. This whole business is an acute embarrassment to me and Cherr-o-key."

"To say nothing of its effect on Mr. Swartz," Wolfe observed dryly.

"What? Oh—the man who was killed. Awful thing. But I don't see the connection between that and our problem. Anyway, Mills told me you hadn't gotten anywhere yet."

"Sir, where were you yesterday between four and six P.M.?" Wolfe asked.

"What kind of question is that?" Foreman snorted.

"A direct one."

"All right, but what's behind it?"

"Dad, that's around the time that guy was killed," Arnie cut in. "Wolfe's pumping you to see if you've got an alibi. Like I said before, let's—"

"Arnold, I *know* he's pumping me, goddammit. I'm capable of speaking for myself." The old man turned away from Arnie and looked at Wolfe through narrowed eyes. "All right, I'll play along; I don't have an alibi for that time, and if I had, I wouldn't use it. What do you think of that?"

"Same with me—I don't have an alibi," Steve said cockily.

"Me neither," Arnie added, grinning.

Wolfe scowled, then let his glance rest on each of them in turn, starting and ending with Acker. "Do you believe that someone at Mills/Lake/Ryman was passing information about Cherr-o-key advertising to the rival agency?" he asked.

"Hell, yes—how else could they get it?"

"Were you satisfied with the quality of advertising that you were getting?"

Foreman crossed one leg over the other and screwed up his face. "Shoot, I've never been satisfied with the advertising I've gotten. If you want my opinion on this—and I know you didn't ask for it—I think today's advertising people are devoid of imagination. Everything's derivative, derivative, derivative. They've gotten so damn cute and clever and precious that they've lost sight of the goal—to move the product." He hit his palm with his fist.

"Amen to that," Steve said. His smirk had returned. His father ignored him and went on.

"I'm a pretty fair-sized account for any agency—not the biggest around by any means, but a healthy piece of change nonetheless. Has this gotten me good advertising, though?"

"Before the imbroglio over the idea thefts, had you been happy with M/L/R's work?" Wolfe asked.

Foreman shrugged. "So-so. One or two spots showed some glimmers of creativity."

"What about the Super Bowl commercial?"

"It was . . . all right, for an extravaganza. God knows it cost me enough. Not the kind of thing you can do regularly, though. That minute shot a pretty good hunk of our annual advertising budget."

"Were you contemplating changing agencies?"

"I'm *always* contemplating changing agencies. It's no secret that I'm known to be a tough client, and that's fine with me. Clients ought to be tough and demanding—that's the only way you get good work. Don't your clients expect a lot out of you? From what I've heard about what you charge, they should."

"I charge what I'm worth," Wolfe said.

"But you haven't figured out yet what's going on between those two agencies." Foreman chuckled and held up a hand. "But then, I can appreciate that you haven't had much time so far. What's Mills paying you?"

"You know better than to expect an answer to that, sir."

"Hah—still cagey, eh? The reason I'm asking is that I'll top him. Hell, in effect I'm going to end up footing your bill anyway. They'll just find a way to hide it in their billings, anyway. They're all a bunch of bandits."

"You seem to have a low opinion of advertising agencies."

Foreman cackled again. "Who better to know than me? I've used enough of 'em over the years. Anyway, how about it? I'll go fifty percent above what Mills is paying you."

Wolfe drank beer and dabbed his lips with a handkerchief. "Why seek to hire me when I already am engaged in attempting to find out the very thing you wish to learn?"

"Dad, it's time for your pills," Steve said, pointing to his wristwatch.

"Oh, hell, I guess it is," Foreman grumbled, pulling a pillbox out of his vest pocket. "Can I trouble you for a glass of water?"

I did the honors, getting chilled water from the carafe on our serving bar that Fritz refills before guests arrive. I handed the glass to Foreman, who nodded and popped two capsules and a tablet into his mouth.

"Sorry," he said to Wolfe, "it's part of the price of getting old. Anyway, you asked why I should want to hire you; good question. The answer is that I've got more at stake in this so-called espionage business than some piddling ad agency. Those guys—and women—are always jumping from shop to shop, merging and folding and starting new agencies every time you turn around. They're like gypsies. I'm willing to bet that Mills/Lake/Ryman won't even be in business five years from now. The partners all will have gone someplace else. But with me, Cherr-o-key is it—the company's my life now. I'm in it for the long haul—as long as I live, anyway. Then it's up to those two." He twitched his head in the direction of Arnie and Steve.

"Nobly expressed," Wolfe said. "But you've done your share of jumping around, too."

"True enough. But that was years ago, when I was a young buck. I've had Cherr-o-key for more than twenty years now, and it's been my only enterprise for almost that whole time. You seem to know a lot about me, more than you let on at first," Foreman said, leaning forward and resting his elbows on his knees. "Well, you probably also know that I'm part Cherokee—a quarter, to be precise, although I feel like it's more. They're the greatest of the tribes."

"So it has been said," Wolfe nodded.

"Anyway, this you probably *don't* know—almost nobody does, and I want to keep it that way: I give thirty percent of the company's profits to various Cherokee groups—both in North Carolina and Oklahoma. Not all of them were forced out of Carolina in the 'Trail of Tears.' "

"I am aware of that."

"Glad to hear it. You mentioned the word 'obsession' earlier. Well, I do have an obsession, and it's to see that the Cherokees keep on getting the kind of financial help we're giving them now. For that to happen, we've got to keep moving one hell of a lot of Cherr-o-key. As far as I'm concerned, every bottle or can of AmeriCherry sold means one less for us. Anything that hurts the brand hurts the tribe, and this damn business with the advertising, to say nothing of the stinking publicity, has the potential to hurt the brand—a lot. All that's a long-winded way of saying I've got more at stake here than M/L/R does, whatever they tell you. So that's why I want to hire you. Plus the fact that you're damn good, and you've got a reputation for keeping your mouth shut. I know—I've checked you out."

"The vote of confidence is reassuring," Wolfe said, pouring beer. "However, I have a covenant with Mr. Mills and his organization, and I intend to honor it."

"All right, dammit, I can't argue against that kind of loyalty without being a hypocrite. I hope you find the bastard who's doing this. One thing is sure—and I've already told Mills this—when I learn who it is, the agency's going to have one hell of a lot of explaining to do."

"I repeat an earlier question: Are you convinced the culprit is an agency employee?"

"And I repeat my answer: Who else would it be?"

Wolfe rubbed the side of his nose with a finger and pondered the far wall. "When the agency presents new advertising ideas to you, who is in attendance from Cherr-o-key?"

"Me, of course—I'm always there," Foreman said with a touch of belligerence. "And usually both Stephen and Arnold here. Arnold functions as our advertising director."

"Who decides to accept, or reject, the advertising from the agency?"

Foreman smiled. "I could give you all sorts of bull-feathers about it being a joint decision, made after a lot of discussion. But that's not how it works, right boys?"

Arnie laughed, but there was no happiness in the sound. "Dad decides, plain and simple," he said. Steve merely nodded.

"But neither one of you is shy about saying what you think of the work," Foreman put in.

"Damn right," Arnie said. "Steve's favorite comment is 'Dreck!' "

"And *your* favorite comment is an obscenity!" Steve laughed, pointing at his brother. They were a charming couple.

Wolfe made a face. "So you three are the only ones to whom the agency presents the proposed advertising?"

"That's it," Foreman said, slapping his palms on his legs. "So you see, the leak has to be at that agency. And I hope to heaven you find it fast—for Mills's sake as well as Cherr-o-key's. Because I'm this close to sacking them." He held his thumb and his index finger an inch apart and jabbed them for emphasis, then stood abruptly. "Well, I'm sorry we can't do business," he said lightly. "The loss is yours."

"That well may be," Wolfe murmured, returning to his book as I ushered Foreman and his sons down the hall. "What about my gun?" Arnie said as we reached the front door and they put their coats on.

"Easy, I've got it right here," I told him, drawing it from my pocket and removing the magazine.

"Hey, I want the bullets, too," he said.

"You'll get them. Put the gun in your holster first." He did, reluctantly, and I handed him the ammunition, which he snatched without thanks and jammed into an overcoat pocket. "I hope he's got a license for that artillery," I said to his father. "Otherwise, some time he might find himself in what our esteemed leader in Washington has on occasion referred to as 'deep do-do.' "

Foreman the elder harrumphed and mumbled something to the effect that he appreciated our hospitality, and the three went out into the gray twilight, where a burgundy-colored limousine idled at the curb.

"You're a tricky one, you are," I said to Wolfe when I got back to the office. "You let me read you that stuff about Foreman that I got from Lon when you already knew a bushel more about him. Where'd you get the goodies about the trucking company and the airline?"

He set down his book and gave me his Grade-A smug look. "An article in the *Times* Sunday Magazine two years ago last fall, probably in late November."

Okay, so he was showing off, but even after being around him all this time, I was impressed. "That's pretty good," I told him. "I suppose you can recall what the layout looked like, too."

"Of course. Archie, as I've told you before, what I read, I remember," he said, picking up his book again. He's impressive, but he's also insufferable.

TWELVE

The balance of Wednesday is barely worth mentioning, other than to note that Wolfe decided to take a break from his strenuous labors. After the departure of the Foreman Three, he (a) ignored or deflected my attempts to talk about the case, (b) made his usual two-hour afternoon visit to the orchids, (c) burrowed into his book before dinner, and (d) plunged right back into the book when we were back in the office with coffee.

Finally, just before I left for a postprandial bridge game at Lily's apartment, he gave in to what he calls my "badgering" and allowed as to how it would be a good idea if I paid a visit to Harlowe Conn, the "Gray Eagle" up on Madison Avenue. Which is why, at ten o'clock Thursday morning, I went to a nondescript modern building on Madison in the Forties and was in the chrome-and-salmon reception area of the executive suite at Colmar & Conn, an advertising agency which, I learned from the elevator starter, occupies a full eight floors and part of a ninth.

"I'm sorry, sir," the tight-lipped receptionist with half-glasses had told me primly, not sounding the least bit sorry, "but Mr. Conn sees no one without an appointment."

"I understand," I told her, smiling like an encyclopedia salesman, "but he might like to know I'm here." I handed her my eggshell-colored calling card, the one that in addition to my name has "Office of Nero Wolfe" engraved in the lower left-hand corner. She considered it, sniffed, and said, "I'll see that Mr. Conn gets this."

"Fine. I'll wait."

"I don't know that Mr. Conn is even in at the moment." Her tone would have frozen halibut.

"I'd appreciate it if you could find out," I replied, still using the encyclopedia salesman's smile. Realizing she was stuck with me, Tight Lips left her desk and bustled through a door to some inner sanctum, returning less than a half-minute later.

"I gave it to his secretary," she said, obviously offended that I had forced her to leave her post unguarded.

I sat for five minutes flipping through a glossy, oversized brochure titled "The Many Worlds of Colmar & Conn," which was filled with color photos of magazine and TV advertising for their clients, most of whom seemed to be *Fortune* 500 companies. I was admiring pictures of a commercial for a sports car that was shot in the Swiss Alps when a tall, slender blonde of indeterminate age wearing a tailored beige suit emerged through the inner sanctum doorway.

She walked up to me, smiling. "Mr. Goodwin? I'm Adrian, Mr. Conn's secretary. He can see you now; I'll show you the way."

I said thank you and followed her, winking at Tight Lips, who frowned and quickly looked away, busying herself with the *Times* crossword puzzle. "Mr. Conn wasn't expecting you, so he had to juggle a couple of meetings, which is why you were kept waiting," Adrian said, still smiling. "He's sorry for the delay."

"It's I who should apologize, for coming unannounced," I said, neglecting to add that I purposely had not phoned for an appointment. I like to keep the element of surprise in my arsenal.

Conn's office alone was worth the trip from Thirty-fifth Street. It occupied a corner, of course, with three windows on each outer wall, and unlike Rod Mills's lair it was big enough to hold at least eight billiard tables. In fact, Conn's mahogany desk, placed diagonally in the outer corner, was every bit as big as the pool table in Saul Panzer's apartment. And Conn himself had all the appearance of someone who belonged behind a desk that size.

As I entered, he stood and circled the paper-free desk, hand extended. "Ah, the famous Archie Goodwin, associate of the famous Nero Wolfe. I'm Harlow Conn," he said, flashing a practiced grin. He was six-three, and although his double-breasted blue suit surely was custom-made to show him in the best light, he nonetheless looked as if he worked out every day. His sculpted hair was as white as fine bond paper, contrasting nicely with a tan that I later found out came from God's own sunlamp, Caribbean variety.

"Quite a layout," I told him, admiring a paneled wall of pictures that included shots of him with two Presidents, both Republican, a Chairman of the Joint Chiefs of Staff, and three of the best-known pro golfers.

"A necessary evil," he explained, dismissing his surroundings with a wave of the hand and motioning me to a small conference table with upholstered swivel chairs. "It's meant to impress clients—and especially *potential* clients," he added with a self-deprecating chuckle as we got seated. "We like to make 'em think we're successful. Will you have coffee?"

I declined politely and started to tell him why I'd come, but he beat me to it. "I've read the papers," he said. The smile disappeared. "I suppose you're here because of . . . what happened to Andy?"

"In a way, but—"

"Terrible, just terrible." He shook his head and stared at the inlaid tabletop. "He was like a son to me. Brilliant. And God, what incredible energy and enthusiasm. The police were here, of course, and I told them I could think of no reason anyone would want to kill Andy. It had to be somebody like a junkie breaking in thinking no one was home. God knows, there's probably enough of 'em roaming around down there in the Village."

"There was no indication of forcible entry. And his wallet—and the money in it—wasn't taken."

"That's right—you were the one who found the—who found *him*, weren't you?"

"Yes. And as you know, the woman who was with me works for Mills/Lake/Ryman."

"Umm, I read that." Conn nodded and fingered a cuff.

"Mr. Conn, Andrew Swartz worked on the Ameri-Cherry account, correct?"

"Yes, and he did one hell of a job for them." He crossed his arms on the tabletop and set his impressive jaw.

"And as you also know from the paper, and maybe from the police as well, the people at Mills/Lake/Ryman believe your agency was learning about their work for Cherr-o-key in advance and adapting it for your client."

Conn seemed unfazed. "Mr. Goodwin," he said evenly, "I don't have to tell you this, but because of your reputation and Nero Wolfe's, I will. Inspector Cramer of Homicide was here yesterday afternoon to see me. He in essence said what you just did. And I will tell you what I told him, and what I am also telling the media: We have one of the finest creative departments in the history of American advertising, and the day we descend to the level of stealing other people's work—particularly that of an agency like Mills/Lake/Ryman—is the day I walk out that door and take the elevator to the street, never, ever to return."

Conn said that with a straight face, so I kept mine straight, too. "You know that Swartz called that woman he knew at M/L/R and said he had to talk to her about 'the cherry drink business.' "

"So she says."

"I believe her."

Conn smiled indulgently, crossing his arms. "It's your job to believe her. After all, she works for your client. Mr. Goodwin, I now know, because of the tragedy of Andy's death and the resulting publicity, that you and Mr. Wolfe were hired to, in effect, find our agency"—he spread his arms and looked at the ceiling—"guilty of idea theft. This is a serious charge to level at an organization whose raison d'être is creativity. And that charge may be actionable."

"If your agency did not steal—or at least adapt—

ideas that M/L/R was developing, how is it that your advertising in two cases was incredibly similar to what they had been working on?"

Conn leaned back and fixed his eyes on me, unblinking. "You realize of course that I don't have to discuss any of this with you?" he said, his tone still nonthreatening.

"Yes, I realize that. But given Mr. Wolfe's reputation, which you alluded to a moment ago, it may be to your advantage to cooperate with us."

"Is that a threat?" he asked with a smile.

"No more than your suggestion that our investigation might be actionable."

"Touché," he said, struggling to maintain the smile. "All right, I'll answer your question, even though I'm under no obligation to do so. First off, who says what we did was 'incredibly similar' to stuff M/L/R was working on?"

"Our client."

"Precisely. You've only been getting one side of the story."

"Which is why I'm here."

"Then it's time you got the other side. M/L/R is frustrated right now. Hell, I would be too, if I were them. AmeriCherry is the category leader in cherry-flavored drinks and has been for as long as I can remember. A couple years back, maybe three, M/L/R got the Cherr-o-key business, and the reason, or so we've heard via the grapevine and read in *Advertising Age*, was they promised Acker Foreman that they could put his brand at the top of the heap. Well, they haven't; in fact, Cherr-o-key hasn't gained a single share point against AmeriCherry in the last two years, and Foreman, hardly a patient fellow as I'm sure you know, is probably getting ready to change agencies again.

"So what happens?" Conn continued. "Obviously, M/L/R sees the account slipping away and they panic, yelling that we've lifted their ideas in an attempt to buy them more time with Foreman."

"Sounds pretty implausible," I countered. "After all, early on, Acker Foreman sees all the advertising the agency has prepared for Cherr-o-key—he's got to approve it. So when *your* advertising came out on television and wherever else, he must have had a pretty good idea that it had been swiped or leaked. And all that's going to do is make him angry at M/L/R."

"Mr. Goodwin, creativity is a funny thing. I've been in this crazy business a lot of years, and more than once I've seen competing brands come out with remarkably similar advertising," Conn said, switching gears smoothly. "Let me give you a case in point: We had a soap account . . . oh, it's been fifteen years ago or more now, and we put together a TV campaign that referred to the brand being 'as gentle as a mother's lullaby.' Almost simultaneously, the brand's major competitor came out with a television commercial with a jingle that included the words 'soft as a serenade.' We never suspected the other agency of stealing from us and, as far as I know, they didn't think we were idea-thieves, either."

"As you said earlier, you have no theories on why Swartz was murdered?" I asked.

Conn shook his head and studied the table again. "None. And I gather the police don't either—or if they do, they didn't bother sharing them with me."

"What kind of an employee was he?"

"A damn good one," Conn said. "Creative, worked hard, put in long hours—although, hell, that comes with the territory in this business. And he was damned ambitious, which I like to see."

"Ambitious to the point of wanting to climb over other people?"

"Umm, well, I wouldn't necessarily term it that way. He was always after more money, though," Conn said with a grin. "I think he wanted to be a millionaire before he was thirty-five."

"And did you give him more money?"

"He got his share of raises and bonuses, and then some."

"Enough to satisfy him?"

Conn laughed. "As much as a guy like Andy could be satisfied, I guess. He had, shall we say, unlimited confidence in his abilities, and wasn't reluctant to point out his successes to his superiors."

"Were you ever worried about losing him to some other agency?" I asked.

"That's always a peril in this business. And, yes, I'd have to say that in Andy's case, that concern did come up in discussions among management. But as far as I know, Andy wasn't contemplating leaving us. He never mentioned other job offers to me, anyway."

"How did his co-workers view him?"

Conn moved forward in his chair and took a deep breath. "Andy was a live wire. His personality was such that he could get away with self-congratulation without seeming arrogant, probably because he also knew how to make fun of himself. I never heard a complaint about him from anyone else in the shop."

"What do you know about his social life?"

"Mr. Goodwin, I make it a point to stay out of the private lives of my employees," Conn said, giving me a peek at his pompous side.

"I wasn't suggesting otherwise. But doesn't the agency have social functions from time to time—picnics and parties and the like?"

"Yes, a couple of times a year. Andy normally came to those, too. The police asked me the same thing, and I'll tell you what I told them: He usually brought an attractive young lady, not always the same one. In fact, I'm not sure I ever saw him with the same woman twice."

"No serious relationships?"

"Not that I ever heard of."

"Did he date within the agency?"

"Again, not that I'm aware of. Pardon me, but just what are you investigating—murder, or what you insist on calling idea thievery?"

"Maybe both, if they're connected."

"Nonsense!" Conn railed, jerking upright and smacking the table with his palm. "We've already been over that. Now if you'll excuse me, I've got to get ready to fly to Detroit for Andy's funeral. That's his hometown."

"Just a couple more things," I said, making no effort to rise. "First, I gather from what you said earlier that you don't have a terribly high opinion of Mills/Lake/Ryman as an ad agency."

"You could say that." He had regained his composure.

"Then why did your agency try to buy them?"

That caught him, and he twitched. "Is that what they told you?"

"Let's just say I heard it in my travels around town."

"All right, there's some truth to it," he snapped, making fists of both hands, opening them, and clenching again. "We—I—*did* try to initiate talks, oh, about eighteen months back. But frankly, I got absolutely nowhere with the partners. And Rod Mills in particular was downright rude in telling us to take a hike."

"If you had taken them over, how would you have juggled the two cherry drink accounts? Doesn't that constitute some kind of conflict of interest?"

"Oh, very much so. One brand would have had to go, and that would have been Cherr-o-key, mainly because AmeriCherry is a bigger chunk of business, probably between three and four times greater, although we aren't privy to exactly what M/L/R bills on Cherr-o-key."

"But Cherr-o-key's such a big part of Mills's business. Why would you even want the agency without its top account?"

Conn smiled sheepishly. "Mr. Goodwin, when I spoke negatively about M/L/R a little while ago, I'm afraid I was letting my anger with the way we were treated by them get in the way. In candor, they have some fine creative talents—among them Boyd Lake, Sara Ryman, and that young woman who I understand was with you when . . . you know. Our hope was to buy them basically intact and maintain them as a separate entity, making them a 'boutique agency,' to use an industry phrase."

"Which means?"

"That they would have remained small and would have handled only a few clients, upscale accounts where a special combination of creativity and impeccable taste are required in the advertising—such as with our fine china account, for example."

"So you'd both gain a tony subsidiary and get rid of a pesky competitor in the cherry drink field?"

Conn smiled again, but this time it wasn't sheepish. "You said that, I didn't," he replied lightly. "And as I told you before, it was—is—simply a matter of time before Foreman dumps them anyway."

"Did Foreman know about your attempt to buy the agency?"

Conn shrugged his superbly tailored shoulders. "Can't say. I've never even met the man. But I can tell you this: Word of our proposal must not have gotten out, because there was never a word of it in the ad columns in the *Times, Daily News,* or *Gazette.* Or in the trade papers, for that matter."

"Did that surprise you?"

"Oh, not particularly. Mills/Lake/Ryman really didn't have all that much to gain by letting word of our proposal leak out. At the risk of sounding immodest, we *are* a damn prestigious shop, but in this business, mergers take place every ten minutes. It was interesting about Lake, though."

"Try me."

"Oh—of course, you probably don't know. He certainly wouldn't have wanted to tell you, given the result. A few weeks after our discussions with Rod Mills, I got a visit from Boyd Lake. He wanted to come to work for us." Conn was smug, both in tone and expression.

"But you didn't take him on?"

He smiled indulgently. "No, Mr. Goodwin, I didn't take him on. As I told you a moment ago, the man is a talent—no question. But he has an inflated opinion of that talent. He expected to join us very near the top of the pyramid. *Very* near the top."

"And he's not good enough for that?"

"He's good, I give you that. But I dislike being dictated to, Mr. Goodwin. And I don't like to hear people bad-mouthing their co-workers. Once disloyal, ever disloyal."

"What did Mr. Lake say about his fellow employees?" I asked.

"I honestly did not intend to bring this up," Conn said, again the smoothie oozing sincerity. "But what the hell, you ought to know about the people who have hired you and Nero Wolfe. Right in this room—" Conn tapped the table with an index finger—"Boyd Lake told me that Rod Mills was a pain in the ass to work for and that Sara Ryman hated his guts because he was a Brit and also because he's smarter than she is."

"Did you believe him?"

"Mr. Goodwin, it's not even a case of believing him. Rather, it's, 'Do I want someone like this working for me?' When I made the original pitch for M/L/R to Mills, I did so largely because of the reputations of Boyd Lake and Sara Ryman. Now, having met Lake, I'm glad we *didn't* buy them out."

"Interesting. Getting back to Andrew Swartz, just what was his role on the AmeriCherry campaign?"

"As creative director on the account, he oversaw all the advertising we did for them: TV, print, outdoor, even some of their point-of-purchase stuff—the works."

"Did he come up with the ideas for the 'AmeriCherry crew' commercials and the sweepstakes with the bottle caps that had endangered species on them?"

Conn hesitated for a heartbeat before answering. "Yes," he said.

"And you approved them?"

"I did. I would have had to, or the client never would have seen them."

"Did the company like them?"

Another hesitation. "They . . . weren't perhaps quite as enthusiastic as on some other campaigns, but, yes, yes, they gave them both their blessing, and I think they've been generally happy with them since. The sweepstakes has gotten a lot of good publicity for AmeriCherry."

"Would you term Swartz a talented creative person?"

"That's a silly question, Mr. Goodwin," Conn huffed. He pushed back his leather chair and got to his feet. "Of course Andy was talented—very talented; after all, AmeriCherry is one of our five biggest accounts. We bring in more than twenty million dollars yearly on AmeriCherry. We'd hardly put a novice on it now, would we? Now if you'll excuse me—"

"Were both those campaigns put together unusually quickly?"

"You told me you had just a couple more questions, yet you just keep on spitting them out like a machine gun. You'll have to admit that I've been very patient, Mr. Goodwin, but I really must go now, and I frankly don't see where all this is headed." Conn brushed something invisible from his lapel. "I've got to be on a plane in less than two hours."

"Just two more questions—I promise. What time did Swartz leave the office Tuesday?"

"The police asked the same thing. I hadn't seen much of Andy that day—I'd been tied up in a bunch of meetings. But his secretary says he left early, around four. Said he had some errands to run."

"Is that unusual for him?"

Conn shrugged. "Andy normally puts in long hours, but we're not a punch-the-clock operation here. The work day is flexible—God knows we all spend enough nights and weekends here."

"Can you account for your time Tuesday between four and six o'clock?"

"The police also asked that one," he replied icily. "I was offended when they posed the question and I am offended now."

"Sorry to hear that. What did you tell the police?"

He exhaled loudly. "That I left here around quarter past five—which is early for me—and walked down to a health club I belong to on Thirty-third near Park. I try to walk at least a couple of miles every day," he said, patting his relatively flat stomach by way of explanation, "and I also try to work out a couple of times a week, my work schedule permitting. But when I got to within about a block of the club, my right leg began bothering me—an old college basketball injury. So I flagged a cab and went home; my wife and I live on East Eighty-first."

"So you got home when?"

"About six forty," he said in a still-frigid voice. "And now, good-bye." He folded his arms, waiting for me to get up, which I did, and he followed me out of the conference room, steering me toward the elevators.

He didn't hold out a hand, which was okay with me; I didn't feel like shaking it. But he waited there, silent and expressionless, until a car came and I got in. As the doors closed, the last thing I saw was Harlowe Conn, walking toward the inner sanctum and shaking his head as Tight Lips glanced briefly his way and returned to her crossword puzzle.

THIRTEEN

Wolfe was settled in at his desk disposing of the mail when I returned from Madison Avenue at eleven-twenty. Normally, I slit all the envelopes and stack them on his blotter, ready for him to plow through after the morning orchid session. But when I'm away, Fritz handles that chore.

After getting a cup of coffee from the kitchen, I came back to the office and slid into my chair, swiveling to face Wolfe. "I've been to the aerie and talked to the Eagle himself. Are you ready for a report?"

Wolfe disdainfully dropped the last of the mail into the wastebasket and rang for beer. "Confound it, yes," he murmured.

"Your enthusiasm is electric. For starters, the gentleman in question is every bit as pompous as our clients had suggested." I then proceeded to give Wolfe the usual verbatim recitation, interrupted only by Fritz's entry with beer. As he normally does during my reports, Wolfe leaned back in his chair, eyes closed and fingers laced over his center mound. When I finished, he blinked and levered himself forward in the chair.

"Based on your narrative, I suggest unctuous rather

than pompous as a descriptive adjective for Mr. Conn. Now I—"

He was interrupted by the doorbell. I could have let Fritz do the honors, but I was curious, so I made for the front door, heading him off as he entered the hall. "Thanks, but this is mine," I told him. "I owe you one for taking care of the mail this morning." He did an about-face and went back to the kitchen while I took a gander through the one-way glass.

"This is getting to be a habit," I told our visitor after I'd pulled open the front door. "Is Mr. W. expecting you?"

"No, but I think he'll want to see me," Inspector Cramer snapped, crossing our threshold for the second time in two days. I didn't try to stop him, but I did take the lead down the hall, beating him by a length to the office door.

"He-r-r-re's Cramer!" I said as I went in ahead of the inspector, but of course that bit of silliness was lost on Wolfe, who had never caught Johnny Carson's late-night TV show and likely never would. He looked up from his book with an expression that would have stopped a charging elephant, but it bounced harmlessly off Cramer, who made his usual crash landing into the red leather chair.

"I sincerely hope this intrusion is warranted." Wolfe spoke the words softly, spacing them for effect.

"I'll let you be the judge of that," Cramer responded without emotion. "It concerns your client."

"Proceed."

"We've talked to friends of Swartz," Cramer said. "He had an active social life."

"As do many people in Manhattan, or so I have been led to believe."

"Yeah, me too, although I suspect we've each had about the same amount of first-hand experience," Cramer retorted. "Anyway, one of those drinking buddies of Swartz's that I mentioned when I was here yesterday said that he—Swartz—had been seeing, among others, a woman who works for another advertising agency, but on the q.t."

"Annie Burkett?" I ventured.

"Nope—that was my guess, too. But the guy, he's a bond trader named Chris Morrow, knew it wasn't her, because he'd met her once when a big group, Swartz among them, went out someplace together, sailing I think he said. And the Burkett woman was along with another man. She and Swartz were just casual acquaintances, according to Morrow."

"That squares with what Annie told me," I said. "She mentioned that she and Swartz had been places together, but with different people. So who's the mystery woman?"

"Morrow doesn't know—he never met her." Cramer went into his cigar routine, pulling one from a pocket and jamming it unlit into his mouth. "He says Swartz told him, about eight months ago, he thinks, that he was spending time with a woman who worked for, quote, a competing agency, end quote, and that he was keeping the relationship very quiet."

"Did Mr. Swartz get any more specific?" Wolfe asked.

"No. Morrow says he and Swartz were in some bar late one night and had had several drinks when Swartz mentioned this to him. He told us it never came up again in conversation."

"What about that address book you mentioned the last time you were here?" I put in.

Cramer waved away the question with a thick hand. "Nah, there were a dozen women's names in the book, including his sister in Toledo and Miss Burkett. We checked out the others; four he'd gone out with two or three times each, nothing serious, at least according to the women. One worked for a book publisher; one for an insurance company over in Newark; two were with a big accounting firm—roommates, in fact, and one had introduced him to the other, if you can figure that out. The last two in the book turned out to be his secretary at Colmar and Conn and his aunt in Lexington, Kentucky."

Wolfe scowled and finished the beer in his glass. "Why did you say your visit concerns our client?"

"Because Swartz told his friend that the woman worked for a competitor."

"Sir, need I remind you that Mr. Swartz's employer handles dozens of products other than their cherry beverage? Conceivably, almost every advertising agency of any size in New York has a client that competes with one of the products or services that Colmar and Conn does advertising for."

Cramer scowled. "Yeah, but Swartz spent every bit of his time on the AmeriCherry account. To him, 'competition' meant Cherr-o-key and Mills/Lake/Ryman, plain and simple."

"You are doing a lot of assuming," Wolfe cautioned, waggling a finger.

"Maybe I am," Cramer allowed, "but you're the ones

who are making such a big thing out of the supposed goings-on between the two agencies, specifically the idea-stealing. If that isn't competition, I don't know what the hell is. And it figures that if information really was being leaked by someone at M/L/R, Swartz was its recipient."

"I do not dispute that," Wolfe replied. "Have you unearthed any other information pertinent to Mr. Swartz's death?"

"If I had, would I be here?" One thing about Cramer—he never pussyfoots around or shovels manure, which was particularly refreshing for me after having spent an hour with Harlowe Conn.

"I know you both have been talking to people at M/L/R. Do you have any idea who *might* have been seeing Swartz?" the inspector pressed.

Wolfe threw a look my way that told me to go ahead and answer. "Afraid I can't help," I said. "Other than Annie Burkett, none of the folks I talked to there, male or female, admitted to knowing Swartz."

"And you believed them?"

I turned my palms up. "Look, I wasn't exactly conducting in-depth interviews. After all, the place has more than fifty employees, and slightly more than half are women."

"Mr. Cramer, let me pose a question," Wolfe said. "Do you believe Mr. Swartz's death was a direct result of the thievery of ideas from Mills/Lake/Ryman?"

"I dunno," Cramer said, studying his fingernails. He isn't used to having Wolfe ask his opinion. "It's as good a place to start as any. As far as we've been able to determine, the guy didn't have any enemies. And robbery clearly wasn't the motive, you know that. Nothing appeared to be missing from the apartment and he had money in his wallet. Obviously, he must have known whoever dispatched him—there was no sign either of a break-in or a struggle, and he was hit from behind, so he knew his killer well enough to turn his back on him—or her. And we didn't pick up any clean prints around the place other than Swartz's own, plus those of a cleaning woman who came in once a week."

"I assume the neighbors didn't see anyone coming or going, or at least claim they didn't," I said.

"Hell, they were damn near worthless," Cramer spat. "None of them knew Swartz, except maybe to say hello to in the corridor, even though he'd lived in the building for four years. But then, that's New York for you; nobody knows their next-door neighbors anymore, and they don't particularly want to. Of course most of them may not have been home from work yet; time of death was between about four and six. There was no question but that the blows to the head killed him—at least three of them, according to the M.E."

Wolfe ran his hand along the spine of the book he was reading. "Did Mr. Swartz's two male friends have any enlightening observations, other than the comment about the woman at a competing advertising agency?"

"Not really. They both said he dated quite a bit, but never seemed to go out with any one woman for very long. With him, work—or at least making money—apparently was the big passion. And the women whose names were in the address book corroborated this, to varying degrees. They and his drinking buddies also said he was a hard-driver who was determined to make it big in advertising. Apparently he hadn't made any secret of that. Quite the contrary. One of the guys—

Morrow again—told us Swartz had said more than once he wanted to be a nickel millionaire by the time he was forty."

"In the current jargon, that means five mil," I translated for Wolfe, whose face had registered puzzlement.

"Which gave him ten more years to get there," the inspector added unnecessarily. "According to Harlowe Conn, his boss, Swartz had a pretty good start. He was making somewhere near two hundred a year, but more important, he was in line for a partnership, which would have meant really big bucks . . ." Cramer let it trail off, glowering at Wolfe, me, and his cigar, in that order. He suddenly realized that what he planned as a fact-finding mission to the brownstone had become fact-divulging instead.

"Dammit, I'm just wasting my time here. You sure you didn't run into any women at the Mills agency who played footsie with Swartz somewhere along the way?" Cramer snarled at me. "Word has it that you have a way of getting women to tell you things."

"Inspector, I'm flattered that you think so, but as I mentioned before, Annie Burkett is the only person of either gender at the agency who told me she knew Swartz."

"Mr. Cramer," Wolfe said impatiently, "you have an army of interrogators at your disposal, yet you persist in seeking to wring information out of Archie, who must spread himself across the entire battlefront."

"Yeah, but we both know that some of my interrogators, as you like to call them, aren't so hot. Not that you're the living end yourself," Cramer said, pointing a thick finger in my general direction, "especially when it comes to playing straight with me."

"But Inspector, I *am* playing . . ."

This time I was the one who let the words trail off, because Cramer had risen, flung his cigar at the wastebasket—missing by a foot—and was off down the hall. I followed, but he yanked the door open and was out by the time I got to the foyer, from which I watched him climb into an unmarked car waiting at the curb.

"Well, he left in a huff yet again," I said when I got back to the office. "Did I offend him?"

"Bah. He's been in a perpetual huff for thirty years," Wolfe sniffed. "Get your notebook. I have instructions."

FOURTEEN

Wolfe's instructions, as you probably have figured out, centered on my making another visit to the Mills/Lake/Ryman offices, preferably before day's end. I started things off with a call to Rod Mills.

"What have you learned?" he snapped before I could spit out anything other than my name.

"Nothing concrete," I responded. "I'd like to stop by this afternoon and chat with you and your partners, separately, and also with Annie Burkett."

"Why? What don't you know that you and/or the police haven't already asked each of us at least a dozen times?" I had apparently caught Mills in mid-funk.

"I promise I won't take long with anyone. I know how busy all of you are, but I just need to fill in a few blanks here and there."

"Oh, hell, all right; what about two-thirty? Everybody's in today, although we're still a long way from settling down to normal, if there ever is such a thing as normal in this stupid business. No more visits from the cops this morning, but we're having problems with one of our clients—not Foreman this time. As if we didn't have enough headaches, for God's sake. All we need now is more TV crews tramping around here."

"Is the trouble you're having with this other client a result of the publicity you've been getting?"

"Nah, it's a creative problem—been percolating for several days. But the timing couldn't be worse."

I sympathized and vowed to be in and out quickly. "Our Mr. Mills is a tad grumpy today," I told Wolfe after I'd hung up. He grunted from behind his book, which was the only sound out of him before we went in to a lunch of sweetbreads with truffles and chervil.

Fritz's sweetbreads were magnificent as usual, and my only regret was that I couldn't go back to the office with Wolfe and bask in the afterglow of the meal while leisurely sipping coffee. But duty called, and at two-twenty-seven I walked into Mills/Lake/Ryman's orange-and-tan lobby, my presence actually eliciting a spontaneous glimmer of recognition from Butterscotch-Hair. "Mr. Mills is expecting you." She said it with some enthusiasm this time, giving me a thorough once-over with baby blues that had been visited by an overly energetic eyeliner pencil. Maybe she thought I was yet another TV reporter, scouting not only news but also beautiful young receptionists with the potential to become tomorrow's television anchors.

The route upstairs was familiar now, and as I moved noiselessly along the carpeted second-floor corridor, everything seemed to be calm. So much for appearances. Mills's secretary, the one who had smiled so warmly on my earlier visit, was a long way from smiling as I approached her desk. Exhaustion showed on her well-formed face—probably from having to deal with the twin scourges of the media and the police. She numbly nodded me into her boss's office.

He seemed every bit as happy to see me as his secretary had, gesturing me absently toward a chair while continuing to scan a sheaf of papers. After about half a minute, he looked up and sighed loudly. "You know, these pushy jackasses just barged in here with their cameras and their lights and their barnyard manners. Never mind the fact that we've got work to do, never mind that there's not a hell of a lot any of us here can tell them about the Swartz business, never mind that their disruption resulted in all of fifteen seconds on the eleven o'clock news, in which we're referred to as 'the agency whose ideas got stolen.' Which of course is just great for our clients to hear. What a goddamn shambles."

"Uh-huh. Have any of your clients, other than Foreman, griped about all this?"

Mills leaned back and snapped his suspenders nervously. "Actually, no, they've all been sympathetic, at least on the surface. Two of them called to commiserate and say they were with us all the way. At least that's the story they're telling us now. My guess is they'll begin falling away a few months down the road, after all this cherry drink crap has died down. When the calls finally come, they'll be warm and friendly. And the message basically will be 'You've done a terrific job for us, but—and God, this has been painful—we think it's time for a whole new approach to our product and its position in the marketplace' or some such bull. But none of 'em will ever even hint at the real reason they're dropping us—that they're afraid their advertising will get leaked to a competitor."

"But if the spy gets unmasked, presumably everything will be okay, right?"

"That's one big if. In the first place, once an agency's reputation gets tainted, it's hell trying to erase that black mark. I remember what happened to a shop not much bigger than us a few years back. They had a spy in the house who leaked a campaign to a competitor, and they were ruined—out of business within nine months. Second, there doesn't seem to be much progress on the 'unmasking,' to use your term. You said yourself on the phone that you and Wolfe haven't come up with anything concrete."

"True, but we're working," I said. "I told you I wouldn't waste anybody's time here today, and I won't. Before I move on to your partners and Annie, though, one question: Where were you between four and six P.M. on Tuesday?"

Mills detached his thumbs from his suspenders and slowly got erect in his chair, eyeing me suspiciously all the while. "Hey, I'm your *client,* remember?" He spaced the words, and the tone wasn't friendly.

"True, but when you hire Nero Wolfe—and me, I'm part of the package—among the things you're paying all those simoleons for is thoroughness."

"My God, I'd hardly hire you if I were the guilty one, now, would I?" The tone had gotten even less friendly.

"Stranger things have occurred. Do you have a problem with my question?"

He leaned back again, stretching his arms. "Problem? No, let me think . . . Late Tuesday afternoon, I was over at the offices of our soap account on Park Avenue. Just a routine meeting to review expenditures, and I'm happy to tell you that everything went smoothly. I left them at, oh, five-thirty or so, and met

Dawn for drinks at the Churchill at about six or maybe a little after. Want to check that with her?" The tone had gone from garden variety unfriendly to downright hostile.

"Hey, don't get your back up. I'm only a lackey for a genius."

Mills allowed himself a weary smile as his shoulders sagged. "Oh, hell, delete that last comment of mine. I'm afraid I've gotten more than a little paranoid the last few days. I've got to snap out of that. Anyway, yeah, I said good-bye to the soap folks and walked over to the Churchill. Dawn was waiting in the bar for me, and then we went to dinner."

"Not to worry," I said. "I'd be surprised if you *weren't* a little edgy by now, what with all that's been happening. Mind if I drop in on the others now?"

"Go ahead. They know you're coming, of course. Boyd said he'd prefer to see you first. He's got a meeting at three-thirty; he's up to his eyeballs with a client problem."

"The one you mentioned on the phone?"

"Yeah. A new fast-food chain. Maybe you've heard of them—Graffiti's. We think they've got great growth potential—as in maybe being the next McDonald's. But we're having trouble coming up with a campaign that makes them happy. It's Boyd's baby, and to further stir things up, Sara's been damn critical of the creative work herself. And you can imagine how Boyd reacts to that."

"The chain doesn't sound familiar, but the rest does—the part about Lake and Sara Ryman going at each other."

The adman shook his head and looked at the ceiling. "You'll never hear me say this a boring place to work. Insane, maybe, boring, no."

I did some more commiserating, and then Mills called Lake, telling him I was coming his way, which happened to be all of two doors down the hall. Lake's office, which was about the same size as Mills's, left no room for doubt as to his origins. A British flag at least two feet by three hung on one wall, along with a poster of the London skyline with a quote, credited to Samuel Johnson: ". . . when a man is tired of London, he is tired of life." It sounded good, and I made a mental note to suggest to Lily that on our next vacation we visit Big Ben.

"Ah, Mr. Goodwin." Lake greeted me with a heartiness that seemed forced, popping up from behind a littered desk and reaching across it to pump my hand. "Terrible times, these. Pardon this clutter, but I seem to function best amid disarray."

I assured him that I was used to disarray and planted myself in one of three upholstered guest chairs. "God, you're a friendly face," he said. "It was madness here yesterday—police poking their noses in every ten minutes, although they weren't the worst. It was the damned television crews, lights, noise, pretty people poking microphones in everybody's face and asking the most inane bloody questions. Cheeky bastards, all of 'em. I was fearing we'd see more of the same today, but I guess now we're old news, eh?"

"I wouldn't get too confident. You may still see police and media around here before it's over. Mr. Lake, I know you've got a tight schedule, and I promise I'll take only a few minutes. First, I'd like to know—"

Lake held up a hand. "I will be more than happy

to answer whatever questions you have, but before that, I want you to see something; I'd like your opinion." He swiveled to the table behind him and latched onto a videocassette. "We can play this down the hall," he said, getting up and gesturing me to follow him, which I did. Color me cooperative.

The conference room was done in executive-suite modern, with tan carpeting, the requisite dark Scandinavian table fifteen feet long, a dozen matching upholstered-but-sleek chairs on wheels, and indirect lighting. There were framed corkboards on the long walls, and a screen at one end of the room. The other end of course contained a projection booth, which Lake ducked into for a few seconds, reemerging and sitting on one side of the table. At his prompting, I took a chair opposite him.

"Mr. Goodwin, if I seem distracted today, it is for two reasons," he told me soberly, pressing his palms together as though he were about to confer a blessing. "One of course is all this upheaval with Cherr-o-key, and the second is because of problems with another client of ours. Have you heard of the Graffiti's fast-food chain?"

"Very recently."

He nodded, pleased. "And I think it's safe to say you'll be hearing more about them—soon. At the moment, they have only a few outlets—mainly in Virginia and the Carolinas. But they have ambitious expansion plans, and we here feel their growth potential is staggering. Although they are not a very big client right now, that growth potential could get us away from being so dependent upon Cherr-o-key."

"But there are problems?"

"Indeed," he said, stroking his beard and frowning. "Graffiti's has built its image around the 1950s—the Eisenhower years, if you will. We have used that motif as the central theme of our proposed campaign for them, a campaign that is to all intents and purposes an introductory one, which can be used in new markets as the chain expands across the country."

"That would seem to make sense. So where's the rub?" I asked.

"The rub is that the client isn't satisfied with what we've come up with. And neither are some people here," he added darkly. "I'd like to show you rough cuts of a TV spot we've developed."

"And this is what the client doesn't like?"

He nodded, pursing his lips. "Correct. At least, not *everyone* representing the client likes it. I do think we have at least a little support for this in the Graffiti advertising department."

"I'll be happy to look at it, but I don't see where I can be much help," I told him. "I'm hardly an expert on advertising."

"Ah, but I sense you are a man of uncommon discernment. I would be most interested in your reactions."

"Okay, shoot."

Lake fiddled with some controls built into the table where he was sitting. "Just remember, this is what we call a rough cut," he cautioned. "It hasn't been smoothed out, and it may seem a little jerky and uneven to you, but it's meant to give a client a good idea of what the final result will be before we spend all the money necessary to polish the spot for airing."

The lights in the room dimmed and the screen came

alive with the image of an aqua-and-white Chevy Bel-Air convertible, circa mid-'50s, cruising along a suburban street with a grinning crewcut guy in a V-neck sweater behind the wheel and two young lovelies in skirts and fuzzy sweaters sitting up on the boot in back. The camera closed in on the pair, who began singing, to the tune of "Moments to Remember." The lyrics started something like *"When we drive out to take a break/ for burgers, chicken, or a shake/we will always head straight/ for Graf-FI-ti's!"* The song continued as black-and-white shots of Eisenhower, James Dean, Lucille Ball, Willie Mays, Elvis, Marilyn Monroe, a Ford Victoria sunroof, kids with hula hoops, and a split-level house with picture window flashed across the screen in dizzying succession. The commercial ended with the same two smiling singers going into a Graffiti's, where burgers, chicken, and shakes were shown in living color, along with a giant jukebox—apparently a standard feature in all their restaurants. The closing line, a voiceover, was "The way life used to be—and still IS . . . at Graffiti's!"

"Well," Lake said with a slight smile as the screen went dark and the lights came back up. "What do you think?"

"Interesting. It's . . ."

"It's dated and trite, that's what it is. Go ahead and say so!" Sara Ryman, blessedly interrupting me, stood in the doorway wearing a blue blazer and a sour smile. "And that's why the people at Graffiti's don't like it. Sorry, Mr. Detective Man, but Boyd's been grabbing everybody who wanders into the building and making them see that piece of work in an absurd attempt to justify it. Pretty soon he'll be making the delivery boys from Guido's Pizza down the street sit there and watch it."

"I don't recall inviting you to this meeting," Lake said coldly to his partner.

"And I didn't see any DO NOT DISTURB sign hanging on the door, Boyd," she retorted with mock sweetness. "As a matter of fact, I was looking for you, to find out where the dog-food storyboards are."

"Berg has 'em in his office and you know it," Lake growled, following it with something about rudeness. He got up, stalking out past his antagonist. "Sorry you had to be exposed to that bilge," she said as I rose. "Poor Boyd, he's resorted to polling the man-in-the-street now."

"For the record, this man-in-the-street rather liked it," I lied. "Catchy tune and all, you know? I trust you'll be around later."

She looked at me and shook her head. "I'm always around, even for people who have no taste."

I gave her my own mock-sweet smile and followed Lake to his office. He was back in his chair by the time I got there, slouching and sulking. "That woman can be a twenty-four-carat bitch. I'm sorry you had to witness that."

I smiled. "Everybody's apologizing to me today, and it's not necessary. I've been around conflict before. When I came in originally, I promised to take just a few minutes, and I will. First, can you account for your time between four and six Tuesday afternoon?"

"Are you serious?" He cupped his face in his hands and leaned forward, letting his elbows support him on the desktop. I assured him that I was serious.

"I suppose I shouldn't be surprised. After all, the

police asked essentially the same question—and not so politely, I might add. But then, I'm not their client." I couldn't tell from his voice whether he was offended or just puzzled.

"As I told Mr. Mills, I'm simply being thorough—and among other things, M/L/R is paying for thoroughness."

"Of course, of course, I quite agree. I was at home ill on Tuesday—a cold that had been coming on. I finally surrendered to it. And that's all I really needed to do; one day at home, in bed and all, and I came back here rejuvenated."

"You live alone?"

"Alas, yes," Lake said, turning his palms up. "I've tried marriage, and to a very fine woman, at that. She lives in Scotland now, Edinburgh, and is wedded to a better man this time, I must concede. In fact, our breakup was what caused me to leave England. Too many memories and all that, you know. What you are asking, of course, is whether anyone can vouch for my whereabouts on Tuesday. I stayed in all morning, babying myself. By afternoon, I felt markedly better and went out for a stroll—around four-thirty, actually; the doorman saw me go. I stopped by a local grocery to get some things, and then I walked for a bit. The fresh air seemed to help."

"How long were you gone?"

"I'd estimate a little more than an hour."

"Where do you live?"

Lake gave me a strained smile and passed a hand absently over his beard. "In Greenwich Village, just off West Fourth. And yes, Mr. Goodwin, I've read the papers, so I realize that is very close to where Andrew

Swartz dwelt. Does that make me a suspect in your eyes?"

"Not necessarily," I said, smiling back. "I gather you didn't know him?"

"Correct."

"I thought perhaps Harlowe Conn might have introduced the two of you when you were at Colmar and Conn a year and a half back looking for work."

That shot hit home. Lake drew in air, exhaling noisily, and did some more beard-stroking. "I see," he said, getting up and walking to the door, which he eased shut. "In the U.K., when two parties meet under circumstances that both agree to be confidential, they invariably honor that confidentiality. I have been here long enough to realize such is not the case in this country, yet I continue to forget that. I assume Conn divulged the contents of our discussion."

"He gave me what he claimed were direct quotes of yours."

"About my partners?"

I nodded, and he did some more deep-breathing. "Have you told anyone?" he asked at last.

"Not other than Mr. Wolfe."

"Are you—or he—going to? Tell anyone, I mean."

"I can't speak for him, but I don't plan to broadcast the fact, unless it becomes pertinent to our investigation."

Lake slouched again and crossed his arms over his chest. "You talk as though I *am* a suspect."

"That wasn't intended. But I do confess to being interested in what was said in your meeting with Conn."

"It sounds as if you've already found that out."

"I'd be interested in hearing your version," I parried.

He did the deep breathing number again, presumably collecting his thoughts. "All right. Considerably more than a year ago, I went to see Conn, to sound him out about what might be available at C and C."

"Were you dissatisfied here?"

"Not overly. But there were—and are—times when I feel limited by the size of our shop, personally frustrated. I know Rod loves running something small and cozy and collegial, but dammit, I sometimes miss a big operation, like the one I worked for in London before I came across. That feeling ebbs and flows in me."

"Is it ebbing or flowing right now?"

Lake gave me a crooked smile. "Not much of either, actually. I'm in a passively contented state right now, which you might choose to interpret as a euphemism for lazy."

"I'm in that state quite a lot myself," I said. "Now—"

"Sorry to interrupt, but I should tell you I've always regretted that I went to see Conn. I honestly don't think I could stand to work for the man, even indirectly."

"Because he wouldn't hire you?"

"Is that what he told you?"

"In essence."

"Well, it's true; he didn't offer me a position. I wanted a bigger job and more responsibility—and more money—than he was willing to give me."

"Did you and Conn ever talk again?"

"No, that was it. And as I said, I am more or less happy that things worked out as they did."

"Do you know anyone else at Colmar and Conn?"

"Not a soul. Oh, I've met two or three of their people at ad club meetings and such, but only to say hello and to exchange brief pleasantries."

"Mr. Lake, how would you describe your attitude toward your partners?"

"To use your own terminology, is that question really pertinent to the investigation?" Lake asked, arching his eyebrows and lacing his hands behind his head.

"Not necessarily, but I find that provocative questions sometimes take the discussion in interesting directions."

"Well, you've already stated that Mr. Conn quoted me on the subject."

"Again, though, I would like to hear your version."

"It's somewhat complex," Lake replied, pulling his tie knot farther down from his neck and passing a hand inside his collar. "As best I can recall, I told Conn that Rod was somewhat difficult to work with, although I may have used stronger terms. And I also said that Sara and I didn't get along terribly well, in part because I'm British and she doesn't seem to like Britishers—maybe because of her Irish origins."

He looked at me as if expecting a reaction. "Go on," I said.

"All right. Anyway, as I said, that conversation with Conn was well over a year ago, and I told him what I felt at the time. I must say that since then, however, our overall relations here have improved."

"For what reasons?"

"Oh, it's really been a combination of circumstances. For one, until this dust-up over the theft of ideas, things had been running very smoothly around here—some new accounts, good relationships with our clients. At the time I talked to Harlowe Conn, we were having problems with several of the accounts, and Rod was very testy because of it—and very hard to get along with. Since then, he's become a lot more mellow, which has made things better here for everyone. Of course, that was before this latest business, both with Cherr-o-key and Graffiti's; at the moment, nobody here is what you'd term mellow.

"As for Sara and me, we will never be the best of friends. We are both impatient and quick-tempered, and we're both also perfectionists. But we have gradually come to an accommodation, that little contretemps of a few minutes ago notwithstanding. I guess you could say we've generally become more tolerant of each other's foibles. For instance, I've learned to at least tolerate her caustic humor, and she seems to have accepted the fact that I will always have a British accent and British values and attitudes, some of which she doesn't embrace."

"But you still think she's a twenty-four-carat bitch?"

The skin above Lake's beard reddened. "I . . . I can't honestly say that I will ever really *like* Sara. And sometimes . . . yes—she is a bitch. But a talented one."

"Do Mills and Sara Ryman get along well?"

Lake nodded slowly. "In the main, yes. I've almost never seen a strong disagreement between them."

"So how would you best describe the current relationships among the three of you?"

Lake pressed a palm on his blotter. "Well they're probably about as good as one could expect, given the pressures and tensions of our business and the various quirks in our personalities. Now, as I think you are aware, I have a meeting," he said, standing abruptly.

"One last thing. If I may be so presumptuous as to make a suggestion, I'd go to the police and let them know about your meeting with Conn."

"Why? It's not germane to what's transpired."

"There's a chance they will find out from other sources, and if that happens, they'll wonder why you didn't say something."

"Who'll tell them—you?"

"This is silly," I shot back. "Of course I won't tell them. But Conn might, for instance."

Lake flushed again, as well he should have, for thinking I make it a practice of running to the cops with things a client tells me. "All right, of course you've got a point. I'm sorry I said that. Your counsel is very sensible and wise. Chalk my reaction up to tension and nerves."

"Consider it so chalked," I said, thanking him for his time and taking a left turn down the hall to Sara Ryman's office, where I had spent a few minutes forty-eight hours earlier. She was on the phone and looked up when I appeared in the doorway, nodding grimly and gesturing me to a chair. She muttered something into the mouthpiece about having to run to a conference and hung up.

"Will this take long?" she asked sharply.

I smiled. "As I've already said once today, your firm is paying for, among other services, thoroughness. And I'm being thorough."

"Are you indeed? Mr. Goodwin, this firm is paying

you and Nero Wolfe for one thing and one thing only." Sara Ryman squared the padded shoulders of her blue blazer and drummed well-tended nails on her desktop. "That is results. And I gather your presence here today suggests that you have none as yet."

"I assume that's a rhetorical question, and the answer is, we are devoting every bit of our energy to the problem."

"Sounds like standard answer 1-A from the first chapter of the detective's handbook. Okay, let's get on with it: What can I possibly tell you at this point that will be of any help?"

"For starters, do you and Mr. Lake often go at each other like alley brawlers, or was what I saw an aberration?"

Now it was Sara's turn to blush. "That was unfortunate. It's just that the Graffiti's spot isn't very good. The client doesn't like it, I don't like it, Rod doesn't like it. But dammit, Boyd sticks with the work he oversaw and persists in trying to sell the damn thing. You're about the eighth person he's hauled into the conference room for an opinion."

"Are the two of you often at loggerheads?"

"Often enough. Call it clashing personalities. Also . . ."

"Yes?"

"Well, this is probably not important, but did you know that Boyd wasn't in the office at all on Tuesday?"

"I was aware of it. Why?"

"He said he had a cold. Mr. Goodwin, did you see any evidence that he had a cold when we all came to Nero Wolfe's office Monday?"

I shrugged. "No, I—"

"And did you see any evidence of a cold today?" She sent a knowing smile in my direction.

"No, but lots of people catch cold fast and get over it fast."

"I thought private eyes cut from the *Maltese Falcon* mold were supposed to be both observant and cynical," she countered. "Are you sure you passed the detectives' exam?"

"Cross my heart."

"That's your story. Now is there anything else you wanted to discuss? It seems to me all we've been doing is wasting time—mine and yours."

"I certainly hadn't meant to do that," I said earnestly. "But there is one more thing: Exactly how long had you been seeing Swartz?"

The pause gave her away. To give her credit, however, she recovered nicely. "What in the hell are you talking about?" she asked stiffly.

"I think you know, or are we going to have to dance around for a while first?"

She looked at me, eyes unblinking, for several seconds. No sound came as her glossed lips formed words, but I caught the brief message: "You bastard."

FIFTEEN

After Sara Ryman's incisive commentary on my parentage, she shot me a glare that ranked right up there with some of Wolfe's. "Do you peek through keyholes, too, Mr. Goodwin?"

"When is the last time you made the acquaintance of a keyhole you could look through?" I retorted with a grin. "Let's talk about you and Andrew Swartz."

She bit her lower lip and let her gaze wander around the room. She clearly didn't want to look at me. "I figured this would come out eventually," she finally whispered, still not locking eyes with me. "There's not really a lot to tell, so I don't know why I just didn't bring it up earlier myself."

"That would have been wise," I agreed.

"We met by accident, really," she said, in a voice now slightly louder than a whisper. "It was about eight months ago, at a screening of award-winning TV commercials, and we each had been involved in creating one of the winners. We were sitting side by side in the auditorium, and we just started talking. The result was that we went out for drinks after work a few days later." She took a deep breath and idly fingered one of the blue dangle earrings that matched her blazer's color.

"The attraction was strong—at least it was for me, and I had thought for him, too. Anyway, we agreed from the beginning that because of our jobs, it would be best if we kept quiet about the . . . *friendship*. But apparently I was the only one who honored that part of the deal."

"That's not entirely true," I told her. "As far as I know, Swartz never told anyone your name, and apparently it wasn't even in his address book. He *did* mention to a friend that he was seeing a woman involved in advertising, and you could say I made a lucky guess."

"I doubt if luck is much of a factor in anything you do," she said with what I immodestly detected as a touch of admiration, albeit grudging. "But I'm glad to hear you say that. Andy and I saw each other regularly—several times a week—for about four months. We went to places where other people in our business weren't likely to be. Although one time, a secretary from here was in the same restaurant in Chinatown where we were. I don't think she saw us, though—the place was big and crowded—and even if she had, she wouldn't have known who Andy was. And then one day, it ended."

"How?"

"How? Don't be naive, Mr. Goodwin. He dumped me, that's how. Plain and simple, no violins, no Rachmaninoff rhapsody. We were walking in the Village at night and he just said, out of the blue, 'I don't think this is going anywhere.' I really humiliated myself then; I told him I thought it *was* going somewhere. But as you can guess, I was wasting my energy. It turns out, I discovered later, that Andy had quite a history of this kind of thing. Meet 'em, have some fun, then drop 'em."

"While you were seeing each other, did he ever pump you about your work here?"

"No, he did not!" she shot back, angrily accenting each word by thumping a small fist on the desktop. "Don't you think I would have told him where to go if I thought for an instant he was drawn to me because of that? Never, not once, did we talk shop. You can believe that or not, as you choose."

"I choose to believe it, but if I were you, I'd let the police know what you've told me."

"And if I don't, I suppose you will?"

That made it two shots from partners within ten minutes, plus one slur on my origins, and I didn't like it. "Look, Ms. Ryman, I just gave you the benefit of the doubt. Now that doesn't necessarily call for reciprocation, but a little trust coming from your direction wouldn't hurt. I seem to recall that M/L/R came to us—not the other way around."

"All right, I'm sorry," she said quietly, sounding genuine. "You're right—I'll mention it to the police, although I suppose that will mean more grief."

"Not as much as if they find out through some other source—not me—and wonder why you didn't bother to tell them."

"You've made your point."

"Good. Did Swartz ever indicate he might be concerned about his safety?"

"No, not at all. God knows the last few days I've gone over every conversation we had, at least all that I could remember. And I can't think of a single thing that would be helpful."

"Did the two of you discuss advertising, even in a general way?"

She smiled, lowering her eyes and shaking her head. "That's the funny part; we scrupulously avoided the entire subject, I suppose for fear one of us would inadvertently slip and say something about work we were doing for our respective cherry drinks."

"Why do you think he called Annie Burkett the other day?" I asked.

"I can only guess it was to tell her who was supplying his agency with information about our Cherr-o-key work," she said glumly.

"Were you surprised when Annie told you about the call?"

"You're damn right I was. I had all that I could do to keep my composure. Remember, Annie knew nothing about my having gone out with Andy. But it was natural for her to tell me about the call; after all, I *am* her immediate superior. I think I'd pulled myself together pretty well by the time we went into Rod's office, though, and found you there."

"I'd have to agree," I said. "You seemed fine to me, although maybe a tad too quick and emphatic in denying that you knew Swartz. Were you puzzled that he didn't call *you* instead of Annie?"

"No. After he kissed me off, I told him in damned blunt terms that I didn't expect to hear from him again under any circumstances. I really blasted him."

"Did you know that he knew Annie?"

She nodded. "He mentioned to me once during our short relationship that he'd run into one of my coworkers a few times in the past on group outings, with several couples, that sort of thing. I don't think he ever saw her during the time we went out, though. I gathered one of his former dates was a friend of Annie's."

"One more point and I'll be on my way. Can you account for your time Tuesday afternoon, say from four o'clock on?"

Sara regarded me hostilely. Then she leaned back and closed her eyes. "Let me think . . . Tuesday afternoon. Seems like years ago. Well—it's easy enough without giving myself a headache trying to remember," she said leaning forward and opening a leather appointment book on her desk. "Oh yes," she nodded, running her finger down a page. "I had a meeting with one of our creative teams in my office at three to talk about a new TV campaign for a Caribbean island we represent; it lasted . . . oh, a little over an hour, I think."

"And then?"

She peered into the book again and wrinkled her nose. "Hmm . . . I see I had down at four an appointment with a young woman who was coming in for a job interview, but she canceled. Didn't give a reason, but my guess is she landed someplace else. Oh, now I remember: I was happy about the cancellation, because I had the rest of the day clear, which is a rarity for me. I went shopping at Bloomies for a birthday present for my sister—before you ask, I bought her a mauve sweater—and then I went on home."

"Were you with anybody who can vouch for you between the time you left here and, say, six o'clock?"

"Nope," she said fliply, "unless you count the Bloomie's salesgirl, who I was with for every bit of ten minutes. And when I got home, I stayed in all evening."

"Where do you live?"

"Upper West Side. And to answer your next question before you ask it, the building doesn't have a doorman. So there you are, no alibi." She turned her palms up and smirked at me, as if daring me to ask if she had bumped off Swartz.

"There I am indeed," I said, getting to my feet. "What would you say if I asked whether you visited Andrew Swartz Tuesday evening?"

Another smirk, along with an arching of eyebrows. "I would say no."

"Well, then, I think that's all. If I remember right, Miss Burkett's office is to the left and then around the corner to the right, right?"

"Right," Sara Ryman said with conversation-ending finality, swiveling in her chair and bending over some artwork on a large table behind her desk. I nodded at the back of her head, wondering if Cramer would ever hear from her, then made myself a three-to-two bet the call would be made and headed for Annie's office. She was putting on her coat when I looked in from the hall. "Hi, can I see you?" I said. "I promise I'll only stay a minute."

"Oh, Mr. Goodwin—Archie! I was just getting ready to go to a doctor's appointment."

She looked as if she could use a doctor, or a vacation, or maybe both. The last couple of days obviously had weighed heavily on Annie Burkett. Her face showed unmistakable signs of strain and fatigue.

"I'll walk out with you. Things been rough?"

"Oh—you mean because I'm seeing a doctor? It's just a routine checkup; I've had the appointment for weeks."

"I was referring to all the Swartz uproar."

"Believe it," she said, making a half-hearted attempt to smile. "I don't think I've slept for three hours straight since . . . you know. I didn't even come to work yesterday, which was just as well. Rod said that between the police and the reporters, this place was a zoo all day."

"Have the police been hard on you?" I asked as we stepped out onto the sidewalk and into a gust of wind that spun Annie around.

"Oh, not really, I guess," she said after I steadied her and she hooked onto my arm. "When they took us to headquarters after you and I . . . found Andy, I got questioned for more than an hour by a man named Phelps, who was, well, brusque, but I guess that's to be expected, isn't it?" She watched my face unhappily for a reaction. Maybe she was hoping I could tell her that Phelps's boorish behavior was a sign that he believed she had no involvement in Andy Swartz's death.

"Brusque is one word for Phelps," I agreed. "Are you going north?" Annie said she was, that her doctor was on East Thirty-third, so I suggested we share a cab, which didn't get an argument.

"Did Phelps seem satisfied with what you told him?" I asked when we were in a taxi heading for the nearest entrance to the FDR Drive.

"I . . . guess so," she said, toying with the buttons on her coat. "I mean, I knew Andy so little there really wasn't much to say, but Mr. Phelps kept asking the same questions over and over."

"Such as?"

She smiled tremulously, then braced herself as our cab braked to a sudden stop to avoid running over a hawk-faced woman in a fur coat, who was walking two

Chihuahuas whose scarlet winterwear featured collars that looked suspiciously like mink. Annie waited until our cabbie quit muttering in Arabic before answering my question. "Such as, 'If you didn't know the guy very well, why did he call you in the first place to talk about the cherry drink business?' "

"What was your answer?"

"Well, I kept telling him that I was the only person at M/L/R he knew at all, so I was the natural one for him to call."

"I assume Phelps asked where you had been earlier in the evening?"

"Yes, he did," she said, a hint of anger creeping in. "Actually, he came right out and asked if I killed Andy. That really got to me. I came pretty close to losing control just then, and I think I sort of shouted at him, asked how dare he suggest such a thing—even though I know he was just doing his job. But the truth is, I didn't really have an alibi for the whole time he asked about. I left the office about five-thirty and stopped off on the way home at a little deli in SoHo to get some groceries, but then I was in my apartment till I walked over to Toohey's to meet you."

"I'll bet Phelps loved that."

She nodded. "He gave me a pretty hard time."

"Uh-huh. And he of course asked what you thought Swartz wanted to tell you."

"Heavens, yes, time after time. All I can do is guess, but like I told him, it must have been about the leaks—it had to be. There wouldn't have been any other reason for Andy to talk business with me."

"Is it possible that he was looking for a job at M/L/R?"

"Huh—I doubt that very much. He probably was making more than everybody in our place except the partners, and he might even have been close to them."

I studied her out of the corners of my baby blues. "You two only met a handful of times as I recall, right?"

She nodded, one hand cupped primly over the other in her lap. "Yes, about six or seven—I've been trying to remember exactly how many. Once we were part of a big group, four couples, who went to see *'Les Miz.'* Also, the same bunch went to a Mets game, and several times, some combination of couples went to movies or dinner. Andy was always with my girlfriend—Lori O'Keefe is her name. She's the one I mentioned who worked for the magazine *Flame and Flair.*"

"Had Miss O'Keefe still been going out with Swartz recently?"

"Oh, no—that was over long ago, more than a year, I think. Which was why I was so surprised to hear his voice when he called the other night. Lori never talked much about it, but I kind of gathered he was the one who ended the relationship."

"Was it serious between them?"

"I think she would have liked it to be, but Andy didn't seem hot to settle down. I could sort of tell that just by the way he acted when they were together."

"Did he ever ask you out?"

"No," she said, coloring slightly. "And if he had, I would've said no, even after he and Lori split up. He's not my type."

"In what way?"

"Too intense. He seemed driven, you know? Even when we were all out someplace, it was like he never loosened up. Always tense, nervous."

"Do you still see Miss O'Keefe?"

"No, Lori moved to Washington about four months back."

"Bad aftertaste of the romance?" I asked.

"Oh no," she said, shaking her head vigorously. "She's pretty resilient. No, she moved because she got a good job with one of the city magazines down there and she sounds real happy."

"On those times you were with Swartz, did he ever ask anything about your work on the Cherr-o-key account?"

Another shake of the head. "Never once, Archie. Mr. Phelps asked me that one about six different times. The subject of work never came up between us, except in a kidding way. Whenever we met, Andy would laugh and say something like 'Whoops, there's the enemy—better be careful what I say!' and then everybody would laugh. It was almost like a ritual."

"And *you* never brought work up?"

"No, I sure didn't. I guess I'm pretty tight-lipped about what goes on at the agency, especially when it involves work in progress."

"One more thing," I said as we spun off the FDR at Thirty-fourth Street, "do you have any theory yourself as to how Cherr-o-key advertising was finding its way over to Colmar and Conn?"

"God, I wish I did," she answered, displaying one of the most honest, open expressions I've ever seen on a woman who is presumably conscious of how attractive she is. "The office has been up in arms over all that for weeks, as you know. But I can't think of a single person at M/L/R who would do such a thing—not one. We're . . . like family, you know? Okay, so that sounds hokey, but it's really that way. That's why it's such a wonderful place to work—most of the time."

"So I gather. Does Miss O'Keefe know what happened to Swartz?"

"Uh-huh, I called her yesterday. She was shocked of course, but she'd already seen it in the *Times*. She gets it delivered down there. Once a New Yorker, you know? In fact, she had tried to call me about it before I reached her. Oh—here's my doctor's building. Let me pay for part of the cab," she said, rooting around in her purse.

"Don't bother, Annie," I answered, covering her hand with mine. "After all, this ride's actually on your employer."

She attempted a smile, although her heart wasn't in it, and she stepped out onto the sidewalk. As we pulled away, I turned to watch her through the rear window, thinking she might wave. But her gaze was straight ahead as she slowly walked, almost trancelike, toward the building's entrance.

SIXTEEN

In the big Webster's Second Edition dictionary that resides on a stand in the office, the first definition of *lazy* is: "Disinclined to action or exertion; averse to labor; indolent; idle; slothful." That pretty well describes Wolfe most of the time. And even when he does rouse himself sufficiently to accept a case, I'll give eight-to-five that he suffers at least one relapse before he wraps it up.

This story's relapse began early Thursday evening, when I returned home from my visit to M/L/R and my taxi ride with Annie Burkett. It was five after six when I walked into the office, which meant that Wolfe, fresh from a two-hour orchid frolic, was just settling in at his desk with beer and his latest book, *The Discoverers*, by Daniel Boorstin. I plopped down at my own desk and suggested he might be eager for a report on the afternoon's activities.

"I am not," came the reply from behind the open book. When I pressed the issue, I got a glare, but a little thing like a glare almost never stops me, so I started right in, beginning the narrative with my arrival in Mills's office. I hadn't gotten more than two sentences out when Wolfe closed his book and rose, beer bottle in one hand and glass in the other, and marched out, taking a hard left in the hall. I could have followed him, but his destination was the kitchen, where, to avoid my badgering, he undoubtedly would get in Fritz's way during the preparation of dinner, which featured veal birds. I made a mental note to apologize to Fritz for saddling him with this king-sized nuisance and then settled back with the sports section of the *Gazette*, which had a long analysis of why the Knicks were dead last in their division.

Wolfe's relapse continued for three days. It didn't bother me the first night, Thursday, because that's when I go to Saul Panzer's for the weekly poker game, and this time, I went home with a fat wallet. But things got tense on Friday. Wolfe came down to the office at eleven in the morning, fresh from the plant rooms, and after breezing through the mail informed me that he was going straight to the kitchen to work with Fritz on developing a new mixture of ingredients for their *cassoulet Castelnaudary*. I let him get away with that one, and of course any talk of business was out of the question during lunch, so it was after two, when we were back in the office with coffee, that I again started to report on my visit to Mills/Lake/Ryman.

"Not now, Archie," he said loftily, "I am in the process of finishing this book."

I told him in Anglo-Saxon terms what he could do with the book and proceeded to report anyway, giving him a verbatim of the conversations at the agency, the set-to between Boyd Lake and Sara Ryman, and the taxi trip with Annie Burkett. At first he tried to read as I talked, but then surrendered and sat back with his eyes closed. When I finished, he opened them and picked up his damn book again.

"Well," I said, "what now?"

"What indeed, Mr. Goodwin?" He gets formal with me only when he's riled, but I was on the riled side myself.

"All right, I'll give you a what: What happens when our clients—you know, the ones who already have thrown a sizable chunk of change our way—call and ask for a progress report?"

Wolfe shrugged. "Tell them what you always do: that we are at work."

"Mrs. Goodwin back in Chillicothe didn't bring her son up to be a liar."

"Twaddle. If I had a dollar for every time I have known you to lie, my fortune would rival that of Croesus."

"You're not exactly living from hand to mouth as it is, although you might be if you keep behaving like this."

The conversation continued in that vein for several more minutes, but there's no reason you should have to endure any more of it. Besides, I made no progress whatever against the forces of sloth. In fact, I got so mad at Wolfe that I ducked out on dinner and walked to a little place on Lexington for a corned beef on rye and milk, chased by two wedges of apple pie. It all went down nicely, but was hardly in the same league with the lamb kidneys and dumplings being dished up in the dining room on Thirty-fifth Street. Such is the price of anger.

The weekend was no improvement. On Saturday, Wolfe didn't even descend to the office after his morning séance with the orchids, probably because he didn't have the stomach—if you'll excuse that figure of speech—to listen to my carping. I finally did grouch at him after lunch, but he played deaf, so I left him with a few choice comments about ergophobia, a word I had just discovered that morning in the thesaurus. As I stalked out of the office, I looked back and at least had the satisfaction of seeing him register surprise at hearing such a word come from the likes of me.

I walked off my funk in the biting January air, eventually finding myself at Saul Panzer's apartment. I rang the bell, and wonder of wonders, he was home, having just cleaned up a nasty little blackmail case over on Staten Island. We ended up playing gin for more than two hours. When I said good-bye, I left behind almost the same amount of lettuce I had won in the same location less than forty-eight hours earlier. Sic transit lucre.

I didn't see much more of Wolfe during the weekend. Saturday night, Lily and I had an early dinner at Rusterman's and then took in the Rangers-Montreal game at the Garden, which our boys amazingly won by four goals. And on Sunday, I also was with La Rowan, at a lavish brunch some plutocratic pals of hers threw out in the Hamptons. This high living in exurbia helped to keep my mind off the case and out of the house until Sunday night. And when I did drag in, the office was dark and there were no messages on my desk.

The relapse came to an end Monday, in a bizarre way. I was parked in the office sipping coffee and reading the *Times*'s sports section at eleven when Wolfe came down from the plant rooms, walked in with the usual "Good morning Archie, did you sleep well?" and eased into his desk chair. Before I could answer—and it was going to be a sarcastic zinger—the doorbell rang. Fritz was out shopping, so I had to pass on the zinger and play butler. Damned if it wasn't Cramer again.

"This is getting to be quite a habit," I told him as I swung the front door open.

"Yeah, isn't it?" he muttered without enthusiasm, brushing by me and taking aim on the office, his unbuttoned overcoat flapping in his wake. Normally, I make unannounced callers cool their heels on the stoop until I check with Wolfe, but given my current attitude, I felt it served Wolfe right to get a little surprise. By the time I reached the office doorway, Cramer already was sinking into the red leather chair, with Wolfe registering neither surprise nor anger.

"Something funny's going on," Cramer snarled. "Maybe you or Goodwin can help explain it."

"I'll help in any way I can, sir," Wolfe replied softly. I knew he was fuming inside but wasn't about to let me have the satisfaction of letting it show.

Cramer leaned forward and laid a thick, ruddy hand on the corner of Wolfe's desk. "I'll take you up on that offer. I got two calls yesterday from Mills/Lake/Ryman, one from Lake and the other from Sara Ryman, and they each wanted to add something to what they'd told me earlier. Interesting, eh?"

"I can hardly be expected to reply without knowing what they said," Wolfe answered, his voice still soft and almost friendly.

"So that's the way it's going to be, huh? Okay, I'll play along. Lake phoned to say he'd once applied for a job at Colmar and Conn. Said he didn't feel it was worth mentioning at the time we talked, but he'd been thinking and decided I should know."

"A prudent decision," Wolfe observed.

"Glad you think so. I hadn't been off the line with Lake for more than twenty minutes when the Ryman woman calls to tell me she went out with Swartz for a while a year or so back. Her spiel was that it had slipped her mind when we had our little chat."

"Improbable," Wolfe said, leaning back.

Right on schedule, Cramer pulled out a cigar. "Damn right. It's also improbable that these two would choose to call me with revelations on the same day without some urging by a third party."

"I do not have sufficient information to frame a response, sir."

"Well, here's a piece of information that you already have. Our friend Goodwin here visited Mills/Lake/Ryman Thursday afternoon. He was there for more than three hours." I wasn't surprised to hear the agency was being watched by the police; what surprised me was that I hadn't spotted them when I entered or left.

"What point do you wish to make?" Wolfe asked, no longer playing Mr. Nice Guy.

Cramer spat a word and started gnawing on his stogie. "You know goddamn well," he huffed. "Goodwin got them both to call."

"Is that what they told you?"

"No, but it's obvious by the timing. It's a hell of a situation when the two of you can turn off and on the flow of information to the police whenever you damn well feel like it. This isn't some kind of game, although to watch you working, one would think so. What I want to know is, how much else have you talked them into withholding until it suits your purposes? This is . . ."

Cramer let the sentence trail off because he realized he now held the attention of only half his audience—me. Wolfe had leaned back as far as the big chair would allow, eyes closed, and his lips were pushing out and in, out and in.

"What the hell!" Cramer said, waving his cigar as if it were an orchestra conductor's baton. "Is he having some kind of a fit?"

"Hardly, although he can't hear you," I told him, trying to suppress the excitement in my voice. "And he'll be this way for a while—count on it. But when he surfaces, things will start to get interesting."

"Balls!" the inspector roared, getting to his feet. "As if I haven't got enough craziness, your boss goes catatonic on me, or pretends to. Well, I haven't got time for this garbage right now."

Cramer barreled into the hallway, with me trailing so close that I could feel his slipstream against my face. I watched him yank open the front door and slam it behind him, sending vibrations down the hall. Then, after seeing him squeeze into the back seat of the unmarked car idling at the curb, I slid the chain bolt on and returned to the office, where Wolfe was still doing his lip exercise.

In fact, he went on for another twenty-nine minutes—I always make it a point to time these things. I plunked down in my desk chair, reviewing all the information I'd laid before Wolfe in the last few days and trying to sort out what triggered his burst of mental activity. I was still sorting when he opened his eyes, blinking twice.

"So." He said it with finality, nodding.

"That's all you have to say—*so*?"

"Confound it, don't mock me," he retorted, his hands continuing to grip the chair arms. "It's bad enough that I've been blind to the obvious."

"Yeah, well believe it or not, I'm still blind, or at least slightly nearsighted. Tell you what: I'll quit mocking you if you let me in on what you learned while you were doing those push-ups with your lips."

I got a glower, but then I got answers, or at least conjectures that made sense. And then I received orders, the kind I like. "I want them here tomorrow night at nine, all of them," Major General Wolfe decreed.

"Yessir. By them, you mean . . . ?"

"Messrs. Mills, Lake, Foreman, and Conn, the Foreman sons, and Mesdames Ryman and Burkett."

"And Cramer, of course?"

"Will Mr. Cramer be back in his office?" Wolfe asked.

"Easily. You were under for quite a while."

"Get him," Wolfe said. "I will extend the invitation."

SEVENTEEN

Cramer was back in his office all right, and some lackey put me right through to him. Wolfe picked up his phone while I stayed on the line. After two minutes of snorting and swearing and trying to pump Wolfe about what he was going to spring, Cramer agreed to show up at the brownstone tomorrow, along with Purley Stebbins. "It's short notice, you know," he grumbled. "You may not have plans on evenings, but some of us do."

"Indeed? Does your attendance here force you to cancel an engagement?" Wolfe asked in an innocent tone. His reply was one of Cramer's favorite words, uttered right before the line went dead on his end. Wolfe cradled the receiver, dipping his chin in my direction to indicate that he had done his part, and that the rest was up to me.

It wasn't easy. Everyone on the guest list—repeat, everyone—already was booked up for Tuesday night, which meant I had to put my powers of persuasion to a test. For instance, Rod Mills, who wanted to know right then what was going on, begged off because of a date at the opera. I said that Wolfe would play genius only in his office and only Tuesday night, and that Mills's biggest client—who I hadn't called yet—would be there. "Foreman's coming?" he said incredulously. "I'll be damned. You talked to my partners yet?" I told him I hadn't and asked if he'd do the honors with them and Annie Burkett.

"It's short notice," he echoed Cramer. "One or more of them's surely busy."

"Under the circumstances, being here would seem to be far more important than whatever else is on their calendars. After all, *you're* breaking a date for the opera. By the way, what do those tickets run these days?" Mills saw my logic and, after making one more unsuccessful stab at getting a preview of tomorrow's agenda, said he'd talk to them and get back to me.

Next I called Acker Foreman's office, knocking twice on the desktop in the hope that he was in town. The knocks worked. The receptionist relayed me to Foreman's secretary, who put me on hold. I waited for two minutes that seemed like an hour, assaulted by the syrupy elevator music of an FM station that apparently is used to punish callers who don't have the clout to get straight through. Halfway through "There Is a Rose in Spanish Harlem," Foreman's gravelly voice exploded onto the line. "Goodwin! What do you want?" Nobody ever said he was gracious.

I explained the plan for tomorrow. "Can't be there—neither can the boys," he spat. "We're flying down to Virginia in the morning for a two-day retreat with Cherr-o-key's regional sales managers at my place in the mountains. Been planned for weeks. Sorry. What's Wolfe got—tell me now." The tone indicated that he wasn't used to being thwarted.

"Hold the line a moment please," I said, cupping the mouthpiece and turning to Wolfe, who was reading. "Foreman. Says he can't make it because of a business meeting in Virginia. Want to talk to him?"

He looked at me as if I'd just called one of his *Paphiopedilum Bellatulum* a posy, then got on the line. "Mr. Foreman, this is Nero Wolfe. Mr. Goodwin informs me you have a commitment for tomorrow night."

"He informs you right. What's going on? Don't beat around the bush."

"What's going on, sir, as Mr. Goodwin told you, is that at nine o'clock tomorrow, I will elucidate on how your company's advertising found its way over to Colmar and Conn."

"Elucidate now," Foreman ordered. "I have the time."

"I do not, nor do I have the inclination," Wolfe countered curtly. "My invitation stands."

"And I have a meeting."

"Cancel it." Wolfe has a pretty good I'm-not-used-to-being-thwarted tone of his own.

I could hear Foreman let out air, then pull it in. He used an obscenity, then did some more breathing exercises. "All right, but this better be worth it, or by God, you'll wish you were back in Montenegro." Before Wolfe could respond, the line went dead and he scowled at the receiver.

"Bravo," I said. "You out-tough-talked him, although you had to be impressed that he's done some research on you. But I'll give seven-to-five he can't name the capital of Montenegro."

That earned me another look, so I turned back to the assignment at hand. Harlowe Conn took my call and sounded surprised—as well as irritated—at getting an invite.

"Really, Mr. Goodwin, this whole business doesn't really concern me in the least, you know. And besides, my wife and I have been invited to dinner at Willard Morgan's."

"Okay, I'm impressed that you sup with U.S. Senators, but believe it or not, this is more important. And it does concern your agency."

"Is Mr. Wolfe going to identify Andy's murderer?"

"I can't answer that, because he hasn't told me—I'm just hired help here."

"And I'm the pretender to the French throne," Conn remarked. By golly, the fellow had an honest-to-goodness sense of humor. "I'd like to talk to Wolfe."

"Sorry, he's not available," I answered. "But he asked me to tell you that a bunch from Mills/Lake/Ryman will be present, along with Acker Foreman. None of those folks have a lot of love for Colmar and Conn, of course, so somebody probably should be on hand to defend and protect the good name of your agency."

That got silence, too, although Conn was smoother than Foreman—I couldn't hear him breathing. And he didn't take as long to dope things out. "All right, I'll be there," he muttered, staying on the line long enough for me to give him our address.

Less than five minutes after I hung up, Rod Mills checked in, saying that Lake, Sara Ryman, and Annie Burkett would be coming with him. "They all had something else to do," he complained, "but I leaned on them. This had—"

"I know, this had better be worth it," I retorted.

"I've heard the line before. I can tell you that Mr. Wolfe has worked very hard on your case, and he is not one to waste his energy." Mills grumbled something about the high cost of private detectives and the conversation was terminated by mutual agreement.

"Well, I got them all," I said, swiveling to face Wolfe.

"Incorrect," he answered, lowering his book. "I called Mr. Cramer. And you turned Mr. Foreman over to me."

"Picky, picky. All right, one way or another, they're all coming. What next?"

"Instructions," Wolfe said. I reached for my notebook and pen, but didn't really need them. This one didn't have a lot of wrinkles or fancy stuff.

EIGHTEEN

Tuesday began uneventfully, unless you count the sleet storm that already was off to a good start before I rolled out of bed. By the time I'd showered and shaved and bounced down to the kitchen for breakfast, the thing was a full-blown traffic snarler. "It is awful, Archie," Fritz said as I attacked my first wheatcake and tried to read the *Times*. "On the radio news, they said many businesses are telling their people to stay home today because of how bad the weather is."

"Look, I know what's really eating you," I answered. "You know that Wolfe has decreed a meeting for tonight, one that might wrap up a case and bring some welcome dollars into our treasury. And you think that if the sky keeps on spewing out ice cubes, our guests might not want to desert home and hearth. Well, put that out of your mind—they're all Manhattan dwellers, none more than a fifteen-minute cab ride away. They'll be here, count on it."

Fritz looked dubious, and as the day wore on, I began to get a little dubious myself. It wasn't until after dark that the storm let up, and by six, it had stopped completely, although the scraping of snowplow blades on Thirty-fifth Street indicated that the fun wasn't over yet.

Wolfe usually adjourns to the office with coffee after dinner, but on those rare occasions when he stages one of his bravura performances, he retires to his bedroom upstairs long enough for Fritz and me to set the stage. This consists of lining up the proper number of chairs in front of his desk, some of which are brought across from the dining room, and of stocking the small table in the corner with a variety of libations.

By the time Wolfe came down in the elevator at eight-forty-five, everything was set. He surveyed the scene, settled in behind his desk with *The Discoverers*, and rang for beer.

"We haven't had a single cancellation, so apparently the elements haven't discouraged any of them," I told him. Wolfe shot a glance at the frosted pane on the window and shuddered. To him, it was unthinkable that otherwise sane adults would consider leaving the safety and comfort of home in these conditions. But then, you won't catch him leaving the safety and comfort of home even when it's seventy-five degrees and sunny.

The doorbell rang first at eight-fifty-six, and I went down the hall to do the honors. It was Cramer and Stebbins, each of whom looked as if he'd just lost a C-note on the Super Bowl. I ushered them in with a flourish, which clearly wasn't appreciated, and stood in the entrance hall as they peeled off their overcoats and hung them on hooks.

"Anybody here yet?" Cramer growled.

"Nope, you're the first, which gives you a rare

chance to exchange pleasantries with Mr. Wolfe," I said brightly. That earned me a pair of scowls before Cramer started off in the direction of the office with Purley a step behind like a loyal aide-de-camp. I went as far as the doorway with them and turned back when the bell rang again. Fritz came into the hall from the kitchen, but I waved him off. "I've got this one," I said, "but stand by in case there's a traffic jam."

Through the one-way glass, Rod Mills looked every bit as glum as Cramer and Stebbins had. This had all the makings of a rollicking evening. "Come on in," I said heartily.

"*Now* can you tell me what's going on?" he asked plaintively as I helped him off with his lined trenchcoat.

"Nope, sorry," I answered, smiling. "This is Mr. Wolfe's show, and he likes to run it his way."

"Well I think it's crazy to keep me in the dark," he brayed. "After all, I am the client here."

"Not precisely accurate," I answered, maintaining my smile. "Your firm, Mills/Lake/Ryman, is the client, not an individual." I was reminded by the look I got that being right does not guarantee popularity. Mills turned in the direction of the office, and I followed close behind.

"Mr. Mills," Wolfe said, dipping his chin slightly. "I believe you know Mr. Cramer and Mr. Stebbins."

"What are *they* doing here?" he snapped. "Goodwin never said anything about police coming. Is this what we get when we pay for Nero Wolfe?"

I would have enjoyed hearing Wolfe's response to that one, but the doorbell rang again, so duty called. This time, there really was a traffic jam. The stoop was crowded, so I called to Fritz and let the hordes in. Annie

Burkett was the first one, followed by Sara Ryman, Boyd Lake, and Harlowe Conn. I concentrated on helping the women off with their coats, leaving the men to Fritz. Nobody seemed the least bit chatty.

"Awful out there, isn't it?" I said to Annie, admiring her light blue knit dress and getting a whiff of a pleasant fragrance that I didn't know. I made a mental note to find out what it was and get some for Lily.

"Terrible," she answered, unsmiling.

"How banal," sneered Sara Ryman, who looked pretty good herself in a brown number. "We're more or less coerced into coming here to discuss grim business, and what do we get first thing in the door but chitchat about the weather."

"It's a tried and true icebreaker at parties, mixers, and other gatherings, according to a book I read," I said with a grin. "Let's all go into the office." Conn, obviously self-conscious in the presence of hostile competitors, dropped behind them. Once in the office, I introduced Conn to Wolfe. He and the other three from M/L/R were as dismayed as Mills had been to find the police present. The women didn't say anything, and neither did Conn, but Boyd Lake piped up.

"The police, eh? So that means we're not only going to have idea-stealing on the agenda tonight, but murder as well, right?"

Wolfe considered him without enthusiasm and sent a sharp look my way, which meant he wanted them all seated. I put Conn in a first-row chair, the one farthest from me, and filled the four second-row seats with the M/L/R crew, Annie closest to me, then Mills, Sara Ryman, and Lake. As is the custom at these soirees, Cramer and Stebbins anchored the back row.

"Who are the other three seats up front for?" Sara demanded.

"Oh, come now," Lake said, tossing his head in her direction and sneering, "you're a better detective than that, Sara. Those can be for none other than the imperial Foreman and his clown princes. And guess which one gets the cushy red chair?"

As if on cue, the doorbell rang again, so I popped up and went to the entry hall once more. Fritz had beaten me to it and peered through the one-way glass. "Three of them, Archie," he said, "one old."

"Ah yes, the fabulous Foremen no doubt. I'll butler them in, you've done your share," I told him, confirming with a look through the glass that a gaggle of billionaires sought entrance. I opened the door and nodded to the patriarch, who was flanked by his scions. If anything, they looked more peevish than any of the others they would soon be joining in the office.

"I don't know why in God's name this couldn't have waited a day or two." Acker Foreman shunned my help with an angry wave of the hand and peeled his overcoat off, hanging it up himself, just like the common people do.

"Damn right," Arnold seconded. "This is asinine. We shouldn't have to—"

"Shut up!" his father commanded, moving toward the office.

"Hold it right there." I addressed it to both Arnold and Stephen. "We've got a little procedure to go through, remember?"

"It's okay, Goodwin," Acker Foreman said, stopping and executing a crisp about-face. "I made sure nobody's carrying weapons."

"Good, now it's my turn to make sure." I patted them both down, first Arnie, who swore quietly, then Stephen, who endured the frisk with his mouth shut, his eyes flinty behind his tortoiseshell glasses. Their father eyed the proceedings impatiently but without comment. "Okay, you can go on in with Dad," I told the brothers.

"Thanks one hell of a lot, pal," Arnie said, showing me his teeth. He was determined to have the final word, and I let him, if only for the sake of moving things along. We all then trooped into the office, Acker leading the way. He marched over to Wolfe's desk and started right in, ignoring everyone else in the room and griping about having to rearrange his precious schedule.

"I appreciate the inconvenience you have been forced to endure," Wolfe said dryly. "But remember, when life's path is steep—"

"Horace," Foreman barked, looking pleased with himself.

"Indeed. From the Odes. The quotation, in full, is, 'Remember when life's path is steep to keep your mind even.' Now please be seated; I prefer talking to people at eye level." The tycoon grumbled some more, less audibly, but his heart wasn't in it. He let his derrière settle into the red leather chair while I directed his sons to the yellow ones on their father's right.

After the Foreman entourage had settled in, Wolfe introduced them to the others, which forced Acker and his boys, being in the front row, to pivot in their seats. That put them at a disadvantage, which might just have been intended by their host. Predictably, the patriarch bristled at the presence of Cramer and Stebbins. "Why are they here?" he demanded, jabbing a thumb in their direction. "Are you an agent of the police?"

"I am not," Wolfe stated firmly. "However, it is possible that some of what transpires here tonight will interest them."

"Huh! And what about that one?" Foreman switched to his index finger, firing it at Harlowe Conn, who flinched.

Wolfe sighed. "Sir, as one who is representing your advertising agency, I ask your forbearance. I have attempted to plan tonight's agenda with some care, and I vouch not to abuse my role as host by unduly prolonging the proceedings."

Foreman continued muttering *sotto voce* as Wolfe asked if anyone wanted refreshments. He got no takers and nodded, leaning back in his chair. His eyes went from face to face, stopping at each for a moment before moving on. "I salute you all for coming tonight," he said, allowing himself a sigh. "You are to be congratulated for venturing forth; this is not weather conducive to travel."

"You're damn right it's not." It was Acker Foreman again, gripping the arms of the red leather chair as if he were anticipating a crash landing. "And by God, I'll hold you to your promise that this won't take long."

"Indeed it will not, sir, unless some among you seek to protract the proceedings. My recitation will be straightforward and succinct."

"And will this recitation tell us who murdered Andy Swartz?" It was Sara Ryman, head tilted, mouth turned up at one corner, and arms crossed over her chest in a classic doubter's pose.

"Your agency—and by extension, you—did not

hire me to denominate a murderer," Wolfe said evenly. "You sought to learn the identity of the individual, or individuals, who were responsible for supplying a competitive agency—Colmar and Conn—with information about advertising that you were in the process of creating for the beverage called Cherr-o-key. I am attempting to discharge that assignment, although I concede that you may not find my conclusion altogether satisfactory."

"Of course they won't find it satisfactory," Harlowe Conn said, gloating, "because there *was* no leak."

"I did not say that, nor did I intend to suggest it, sir," Wolfe replied coldly. "What I mean is, I can only offer conjecture—albeit well reasoned, as to what transpired."

"Hold it right there," Cramer growled. "You mean you got us over here in an ice storm just so we could listen to some of your ivory tower theorizing? And that you haven't got a damned thing to say about Swartz's murder?"

"Inspector, no one compelled you and Sergeant Stebbins to join this gathering. When I called you with the invitation, I made no promises regarding a revelation, although I thought you might find the evening instructive. But you are of course free to leave at any time; I would not want you to think you are squandering the money of the taxpayers of the City of New York by being here."

"We'll stay," Cramer muttered.

"As you wish," Wolfe said, pouring beer and contemplating the foam while it dissipated. "Now, I propose to reconstruct what I consider a highly probable series of events. I—"

"Highly probable, you say?" Boyd Lake asked, leaning forward with his palms on his knees and looking disgusted. "Mr. Cramer is right—this really *is* ethereal, isn't it?"

"Mr. Lake, one of my dictionary's definitions of ethereal is 'characterized by extreme delicacy,' " Wolfe responded. "After I finish, you may wish to cavil about my conclusions. But until then, I beg your indulgence."

"You've got it," Lake said, his expression brightening. "I was privileged to have a superb education in England, but despite that, you won't catch me trying to spar with you over the language."

Wolfe dipped his chin in Lake's direction and made a chapel with his fingers. "Thank you; that is comforting to know. Now to contradict Mr. Conn's last statement, there was indeed a leaking to Colmar and Conn of information about Mills/Lake/Ryman's in-progress creative work for Cherr-o-key. Of this I have no doubt whatever.

"It is clear that Mr. Swartz was the initial recipient of this information, and he put it to almost immediate use in the creation of advertising for AmeriCherry—specifically television commercials and a contest which had as its theme endangered species of wildlife. Whether others in the agency—including Mr. Conn—knew that Mr. Swartz was creating advertising based on his knowledge of a competitor's planned campaigns is problematic. It would seem, however, that Mr. Swartz, presumably a loyal employee—and unquestionably an ambitious one—might have told one or more of his superiors of his good fortune in coming into the possession of valuable intelligence."

"You told me when I went to your office that you

didn't know anything about what the other agency was working on," Cramer said sharply to Conn. "You sticking with that, or do you want to reconsider?"

Wolfe eyed Cramer and then Conn, but he made no complaint about the interruption. Conn turned in his chair and looked back at the inspector. "I wasn't under the impression that this was to be an inquisition," he said, clearing his throat.

Cramer shrugged. "It's not. This is Wolfe's show, but if I find out you lied to us in a murder investi—"

"All right!" Conn said, pulling out a handkerchief and swabbing his patrician forehead. "All right." He took a deep, asthmatic breath and looked around the room as if he were trying to find a friendly face. "I was going to tell you the next time we talked; I assumed I would see you again," he told Cramer plaintively. "I certainly wouldn't have chosen a gathering like this."

Cramer was impassive, a pose he has found effective in the past. My eyes moved to Sara Ryman, who seemed to be taking pleasure in watching Conn's facade crumbling, and I decided at that moment that she was not the kind of woman I wanted to know any better. By now, all eyes were on the war hero turned advertising executive, who didn't look overly heroic.

"Andy came to me one afternoon late last summer, or maybe it was fall by then," Conn said in a low, husky voice as he looked at the floor. "He was very excited, and he said he knew what Cherr-o-key's next TV campaign was going to be."

"Goddammit!" Acker Foreman shouted. "You miserable, lousy—"

"Enough," Wolfe said, his voice cleanly severing the

old tycoon's sentence. "You will have ample opportunity to express yourself before we adjourn." He then nodded to Conn.

"I asked Andy where he got his information," the adman continued slowly, still looking at the floor, or maybe at the toes of his highly polished black wing tips. "He said he couldn't tell me, except that it was a 'mole.' He used the term several times."

"I'm not really surprised at what I'm hearing," Foreman spat, jabbing a finger this time at Rod Mills. "How many times did I tell you that your agency is a kindergarten? You've got slipshod procedures, careless, cavalier employees. A bunch of undisciplined, unprofessional kids without any real loyalties and without any sense of order—or honor, for that matter. Well, dammit, one of 'em obviously decided to sell us down the river to those buttoned-up corporate bastards at AmeriCherry."

"Just a minute. There is no evidence that anybody from M/L/R did this," Mills shot back.

"Mr. Conn has the floor," Wolfe said. "We owe him the courtesy of hearing him out."

"Don't do me any favors," Conn said ruefully, messing up his milk-white hair by running a hand through it. "Well, as I was saying, Andy wouldn't tell me who gave him the information about the new 'Cherr-o-key crowd' campaign, although he insisted the source was dependable. And I had to agree—hell, he told me all sorts of specifics about the campaign."

"And Mr. Swartz suggested that you develop something similar—and before Cherr-o-key's commercials were put on the air?" Wolfe asked.

Conn straightened up and squared his shoulders, trying to regain some dignity. "In effect . . . although I was right with him on that."

"I'll just bet you were," Sara Ryman said darkly.

"Did your client know about the information you had received?" Wolfe asked Conn.

"Not precisely. I told him we wanted to rush this commercial into production because we had an inkling about the kind of campaign being worked up for Cherr-o-key."

Lake exploded. "Some inkling! And they say political campaigns provide the biggest opportunity for dirty tricks."

Wolfe looked at the Englishman without enthusiasm and filled his pilsener glass from the second bottle of Remmers on his desk. "Was anyone else in your employ aware that Mr. Swartz was a conduit?" he asked Conn.

"Not that I know of," he said, coloring. "The two of us . . . didn't exactly broadcast the fact around the office."

"Hardly surprising. Very well, if I may continue from the point at which we digressed: As I had suggested, Mr. Swartz was indeed the recipient of specifics concerning Cherr-o-key advertising."

"Believe it or not, we're keeping up with you," Arnold Foreman said with a sneer.

"It is heartening to know that I merit your attention," Wolfe replied. "Is there anything else you wish to expostulate on before I continue?" That got the desired result, which is to say Arnold sank back into his chair, pouting, and shut his yap.

"Very well. While it was easy to determine Mr.

Swartz's role, it became considerably more difficult to identify his informant. After all, many people, employees of Mills/Lake/Ryman as well as outside contractors, were privy to specifics of the commercial—and later, of the sweepstakes. Is that not correct, Mr. Mills?"

"It is," he said listlessly.

"However, timing is the linchpin here."

"Meaning?" Sara Ryman asked, pointing her chin at Wolfe.

"Meaning that events rarely occur by accident," he said. "When Mr. Goodwin visited Mr. Conn at his office earlier this week, he learned, among other things, that Andrew Swartz was driven by limitless ambition, with concomitant avarice."

"Hardly a surprise, and hardly a sin, particularly in our business," she retorted. "How does timing figure into this?"

"Bear with me, Miss Ryman. Until very recently, Mr. Swartz did not know the identity of his informant. He—"

"How could he help but know it?" Cramer argued, leaning forward and gnawing on an unlit cigar. "You mean their communication all was done by phone? Or maybe by fax or letter?"

"No, sir, I don't mean that, nor did I suggest it. They likely had a number of face-to-face meetings, but the informant insisted—with good reason, of course—on remaining anonymous. And because Mr. Swartz was ecstatic about receiving what obviously was accurate information, he chose not to insist on learning the name of his Quisling."

"Are you trying to make us play guessing games?"

Boyd Lake grumbled, combing his beard with stubby fingers.

"I am not," Wolfe sniffed, affronted at the suggestion. "I do, however, endeavor to paint as complete a picture as possible of the stage as the curtain rises."

"Save us your metaphors, please, and get on with it," Sara Ryman sighed, crossing her arms and rolling her eyes.

Wolfe glared at M/L/R's female partner and drew in air. "If I may continue from the point at which a series of interruptions began, Mr. Swartz did not know who his informant was until recently, and he learned that individual's identity only because of a chance occurrence, something he did not initiate and had no way of anticipating."

"Boy, you sure love to build suspense, don't you?" It was Stephen, the left side of his face twitching.

"Mr. Swartz apparently knew no one at Mills/Lake/Ryman other than Miss Burkett," Wolfe went on as though he hadn't heard a thing. I smiled to myself, realizing Wolfe—that big old softy—was actually protecting Sara Ryman's privacy.

"When he was approached by his informant, probably several months ago, that person may well have represented himself or herself as an employee of the agency, which would explain the possession of such detailed information about Cherr-o-key advertising," Wolfe said. "Was Mr. Swartz suspicious as to the accuracy of the intelligence he was receiving? And was he curious as to why it was being offered to him? The answer to both questions probably is yes, but we will never know. Very likely, however, his eagerness to score a coup with his superiors at Colmar and Conn overrode any wariness or skepticism he possessed."

"Wait a minute," Cramer piped up. "There's a lot of junior agency people who don't make all that much dough. Who's to say one of them from M/L/R didn't decide to peddle information? If that was the case, Swartz wouldn't have been even in the least suspicious. You know damn well that greed and larceny come as naturally as breathing."

"I agree, and I weighed that possibility," Wolfe conceded, "but I have a different explanation to offer. Consider, if you will, that because of his penchant for privacy, Mr. Foreman has a face that is not widely recognizable, and further—"

"What are you driving at?" Acker Foreman said, coughing and leaning forward, sliding his hands back on the chair arms as if getting ready to push to his feet.

"A moment, sir," Wolfe said sharply, holding up a palm. "On the Wednesday before last, six days before Mr. Swartz was killed, the *Gazette* published a photograph of you. Mr. Swartz undoubtedly saw that picture."

"Oh, come off it!" Stephen Foreman erupted, throwing his arms wide and almost hitting both his brother and Harlowe Conn in the process. His face was twitching again. "You're not going to get anyone to believe that my father, one of the most successful, most honest men in America, would ever . . . Why, we can sue you for everything you've got. We . . . you . . ." He sputtered some more, mostly incoherent syllables, at Wolfe, who was unimpressed with the histrionics.

"Am I hearing right?" Boyd Lake said, cupping an ear for effect. "Are you telling us that Acker Foreman leaked the stuff himself? And also killed Swartz?"

NINETEEN

Wolfe leaned back, looking from face to face as if waiting for reactions. The first one came from Foreman himself, who started talking just as Cramer was about to. "This is balderdash, and given your reputation for smarts, you know it, Wolfe," the tycoon roared. "Stephen said something about bringing suit, and although you damn well know how I feel about publicity, you have slandered me in front of a roomful of people."

"You have been accused of nothing, sir," Wolfe answered calmly, adjusting his bulk. "I merely made three statements: One, that you are not widely recognizable; two, that your likeness appeared in a newspaper photograph six days before Mr. Swartz's death; and three, that Mr. Swartz almost surely saw that photograph."

"That's getting pretty damn close to an accusation," Foreman retorted.

"Such was not intended," Wolfe said. "I apologize for any misunderstanding. What I had begun to state before you interrupted me earlier was that you have a face that is not widely recognizable, and further, the same is true of your son, Arnold, who also was in that newspaper photograph."

Like fans at a tennis match, everyone turned toward Arnold Foreman, who retorted with, "What in God's name is that supposed to mean?"

"Sir," Wolfe addressed him, "you had an adversarial relationship with the Mills/Lake/Ryman agency almost from the beginning of its association with Cherr-o-key. Your hostility, particularly toward Mr. Lake, increased steadily, and on at least three occasions, acrimonious words were exchanged. Twice, you angrily stormed out of meetings. Does anyone here dispute that?" This time, no one piped up, although Acker Foreman looked as if he wanted to.

"Very well," Wolfe continued, keeping his eyes fastened on Arnold. "Although your father had expressed growing dissatisfaction with the agency—which was hardly out of character for him—your vitriol was of such intensity that you chose to accelerate the process. What better way to discredit M/L/R than to have its ideas stolen by the agency representing your principal competitor?"

"Dad, we don't have to sit here and listen to this madman," Arnold barked, standing up and starting toward the door.

"Sit down!" Acker crackled. "He may well be a madman—or at least a mountebank—but I want to hear him out. Go on, Wolfe, and it better be good, because the ice you're skating on could be melting."

"I have skated on thinner stuff, and likely will again," Wolfe said as a red-eared Arnold Foreman slunk back into his chair, glancing furtively at his father. "It is clear to me that your son sought out Mr. Swartz, knowing that he was a key figure in Colmar and Conn's creative work for AmeriCherry. He probably told Mr. Swartz that he was an employee of M/L/R, and he likely demanded payment for divulging information, as Inspector Cramer suggested earlier. Such a stratagem would have seemed natural to Mr. Swartz and helped to allay any suspicion he might have as to his source's motivation."

"Goddammit, I'm leaving," Arnold said, but this time it was Purley Stebbins, not his father's sharp words, that stopped him. Purley, hands on hips, blocked the route to the hall, gesturing Arnold back to the chair. Wolfe used the interruption to pour the rest of the beer from the second bottle on his blotter. He drained half the glass and dabbed his lips with a handkerchief.

"Mr. Swartz undoubtedly was impressed by the degree of detail he received about the advertising campaigns Cherr-o-key was planning. As I suggested earlier, he probably was curious about his informant's identity, but not so curious that he would jeopardize what he saw as an already tenuous relationship. Above all, he dearly coveted the information this individual was offering, and if part of the price was the source's anonymity, so be it."

"And where does the *Gazette* photo come in?" Cramer demanded.

"I'm getting to that. Mr. Swartz received intelligence from his still-anonymous informant and used it to quickly develop the two campaigns that both beat his competitor into the media and humiliated its agency. He was praised and well compensated by his delighted employer," Wolfe said, glancing at Conn, who quickly looked down. "But when he saw the photograph of Arnold Foreman in the newspaper, he realized that there was the potential for even greater financial gain."

"Blackmail," Cramer said.

"Yes. Mr. Swartz reckoned that the son was operating without his father's blessing, and he also correctly surmised that as tough a client and a competitor as Acker Foreman is reputed to be, he detests treasonous behavior, regardless of its perpetrator or its target. He then confronted Arnold, threatening to expose him unless payment was made." Wolfe paused to drink more beer.

"This is total crap!" Arnold shouted. "Dad, if you don't sue this con artist, I will. I'm—"

"Continue," Acker Foreman said icily, his eyes fastened on Wolfe.

"Thank you. Arnold at first agreed to pay, but then, for whatever reasons, he demurred. Mr. Swartz repeated his threat of exposure, although instead of going to the senior Foreman, he telephoned someone he knew at Mills/Lake/Ryman: Miss Burkett."

"Why me?" Annie asked.

"One can only speculate," Wolfe said. "Perhaps he had stirrings of conscience, but it is far more likely that he planned to use you as leverage to pry money out of Arnold Foreman."

"How do you mean?" Her face reflected her puzzlement.

"Mr. Swartz telephoned you on Monday, asking you to meet him the next night and saying he wanted to talk about 'the cherry drink business,' correct?"

"Yes," Annie replied, nodding and kneading her hands.

"After he talked to you, he very likely reached Arnold Foreman and told him of your appointment. His intent was to force the payment of what Mr. Goodwin refers to as 'hush money.' "

"But why did Andy have to call me at all? Couldn't he have just *said* we were going to meet?"

Wolfe leaned back and sighed. "That would have been unduly risky for him. What if Mr. Foreman had telephoned you to check on the story?"

"I never even *saw* the man before tonight," Annie argued, looking at Arnold, who was slouched in his chair, shaking his head and rolling his eyes. "Why would he call me? And if he had, I certainly wouldn't have told him who I was meeting."

"Mr. Swartz couldn't take that chance," Wolfe said patiently. "This way, he was covered in the event of the admittedly unlikely occurrence of a call from Arnold Foreman; and if Mr. Foreman had knuckled under on Tuesday and coughed up the money, Andrew Swartz simply would have telephoned you and cancelled your meeting, probably saying something to the effect that his earlier call had been a false alarm."

"So what happened next?" Mills asked Wolfe.

"Arnold Foreman went to the Swartz apartment sometime late Tuesday afternoon, presumably to discuss the threat to expose him. It is possible that during the ensuing conversation, he even agreed to pay something to Mr. Swartz. All of you know the rest: Later that evening, Mr. Goodwin and Miss Burkett went to the apartment and found Mr. Swartz's body."

"You're leaving something out of your little story," Cramer said. "How did Swartz get dead?"

"That was not part of my assignment," Wolfe said, turning a palm over. "As I said at the beginning, I was hired only to discover how Mills/Lake/Ryman's advertising ideas were finding their way to Colmar and Conn." He looked at Harlow Conn as if inviting contradiction, but the Gray Eagle studied his polished shoe tips again and kept his mouth shut.

"Mr. Wolfe," Acker Foreman said between clenched teeth, "you also told us when we sat down that what you were offering us was conjecture. If that is the case, how much, if any, of what you have said tonight can you prove?"

"None of it," Wolfe answered lightly.

"That being the case, sir, I see no further need for us to impose upon your hospitality. Good evening." The tycoon gestured to his sons, who got to their feet an instant after he did and trailed him out of the office and into the hall.

Wolfe turned to me and dipped his chin, his cryptic way of indicating that I should follow them and handle the farewell honors. I did, catching the trio as they were thrusting arms into overcoats in the front hall. Playing my part, I opened the front door. Acker Foreman, looking as if he couldn't leave the brownstone fast enough, gave me a nod on the way out, while Arnold just sneered again and Steve, bringing up the rear, muttered, "Thank you, Mr. Spade." I shut the door harder than I had to, narrowly missing his trailing leg, and watched through the panel as they plodded down the steps and disappeared into the soft lighting and plush upholstery of their elongated limo.

I got back to the office just in time to hear the New York Police Department reaming Wolfe out, which always is worth the price of admission. ". . . and you really *don't* have a goddamn speck of proof, do you?" Cramer was saying as he stood in front of Wolfe's desk, hands on hips.

"No, I thought I made that manifestly clear at the beginning of the evening," Wolfe responded, oblivious to the looks directed to him by five members of New York's advertising community. "But I have surely pointed the way for you."

"Pointed the way my Aunt Sophie," Cramer barked. "Hell, I could've spent the evening back in the office doing something constructive, like reading three-page memos from the commissioner about how the department needs to work on its public image. Let's get out of here," he said over his shoulder to Stebbins, whose face never registered any emotion beyond boredom.

Harlowe Conn used the occasion to get up, too, mumbling something like thanks to Wolfe and heading out without a look at any of the M/L/R crew. Once again, I played doorman, following them down the hall, giving out with a parting pleasantry that was met by glares and silence, and making sure they got safely out onto the stoop. Cramer and Stebbins, who ignored Conn, had a car waiting, albeit a few doors down the street and roughly half the length of the Foreman carriage. As for Conn, he headed east, presumably to flag a taxi on Eighth Avenue.

I bolted the door for the second time in three minutes and went back to the office, where it was Mills's turn to sound off to Wolfe.

"I don't really see that you've definitively identified the leak," he said, leaning forward in his chair. "I admit that your line of reasoning concerning young Foreman makes a certain amount of sense, but how do we"—he casually extended one arm, palm up, in the general direction of his partners, apparently including Annie as well—"know you've got the right guy? I mean, he just walked out of here, as free as the right to vote, and the police didn't lift a pinkie to stop him. Hell, we all heard what the inspector said to you."

Wolfe favored each of the partners in turn with a scowl, then let his gaze rest on Mills. "You do not of course know, at least to a moral certainty, if I have got the right man. Let us assume, however, that no further thefts of your creativity occur. How long will it take for you to be satisfied that my explanation is correct?"

Mills looked at Lake and Sara, both of whom shrugged. "I honestly don't know if Mr. Wolfe has it right or not," Lake mused, stroking his beard, "but I have to concede that the solution he put forth sounds plausible to me."

"Of course it does, Boyd," Sara purred, "especially given your feelings about Arnold the Unsteady."

"Oh, come off it, Sara," Lake snapped. "You know damn well that—"

"This isn't getting us anywhere," Rod Mills interjected sharply. "A legitimate question has been posed, and it deserves a thoughtful, measured answer. Mr. Wolfe, speaking for the agency, I am not yet prepared to pay the remainder of our fee. When you took the case, you said the fee wasn't negotiable, and I accepted your terms—I still do. However, I am not convinced that Arnold Foreman is the mole, as much as I detest the weasel. But, if you are correct and that Swartz fellow was the contact, then the espionage has ended. Assuming the old man still keeps us as a client, and also assuming no other ideas are pilfered in, say, the next ninety days, the balance of the fee is yours."

"Sir, our agreement contained no codicil about Mr. Foreman continuing to patronize your agency," Wolfe retorted, waggling a finger. "However, I recognize that what I have said tonight does not in and of itself constitute total satisfaction for you and your partners. I bow to your wishes, with two exceptions: that the rest of the monies be payable to me in sixty days rather than ninety; and that any decision Acker Foreman makes regarding an agency have no bearing on the remittance of my fee."

Mills and Wolfe locked stares for several seconds before the adman blinked. "All right," he sighed, "assuming Sara and Boyd have no objections, sixty days it is—whether we keep Cherr-o-key or not." The partners indicated their agreement with shrugs and nods, and they all stood up, along with Annie Burkett, who looked as if she could use a minimum of fifteen hours sleep. For that matter, none of the others were the picture of vitality, either. But then, they all had reason to be dragging.

TWENTY

As it turned out, Wolfe didn't have to wait sixty days to get the balance of his fee—or even a week, for that matter. On Wednesday at eleven-twenty in the morning, less than thirty-six hours after the gathering in the brownstone, the doorbell rang. Fritz was out getting provisions, so I got up from my desk, where I had been trying to find an error in our checking account balance, and went to the front hall, took a peek through the one-way panel, and then returned to the office.

"Guess who?" I said to Wolfe, who looked up from his crossword puzzle peevishly as the bell sounded again.

"I'm not in the mood for guessing games, but if I were, my answer would be Inspector Cramer," he responded sourly.

"Bingo. I assume I let him in?"

Getting no response, which I took to be a yes, I marched back down the hall and pulled open the door, expecting a surly remark. Wrong. "Good morning, Archie," Cramer said as he stepped in out of the flurries. I start worrying when he uses my Christian name, because it indicates either that he wants a favor or that something good has happened from his point of view, which frequently means something bad has happened from ours.

"Is Wolfe at his desk?" he asked as he pulled off his overcoat. Another bad sign—he normally barrels past me without asking. I answered in the affirmative and followed him to the office, where he as usual parked his broad beam in the red leather chair, causing the cushion to sigh.

Wolfe set his puzzle down, breathed deeply, and looked at Cramer quizzically, saying nothing.

"I've got some news about the Swartz case," the inspector said evenly, pulling a cigar from his breast pocket.

"Indeed?"

"Yeah, indeed. You had it nailed. This morning, around eight-fifteen, who marches into headquarters but Acker Foreman himself, with son Arnold in tow, and Arnold doesn't look so hot, more than a little bit peaked to say the least. No lawyer, just the two of 'em—damnedest thing I've ever seen. Anyway, the old man says Arnold has come to make a statement about how he hit Swartz over the head with that piece of marble. And by God, he does, lays the whole thing out. I think he's more frightened of his father than of the prospect of being a guest of the state for the rest of his days. It was pretty much like you said the other night: Arnold hated the people at the agency, particularly the Englishman, and he found out that Swartz was one of the key people working on the rival cherry drink's advertising.

"He got hold of Swartz, told him he held some sort

of minor administrative slot at Mills/Lake/Ryman, that he was grossly underpaid by the agency, and that for a price he would spill advance information about Cherr-o-key advertising. Swartz, who apparently didn't know anybody at M/L/R other than Miss Burkett and of course Miss Ryman, was suspicious at first. He asked his name, but Arnold refused with good reason to give out any moniker—hell, Swartz could have called the agency and checked it then. So to show good faith, Arnold told him in detail about an upcoming Cherr-o-key TV commercial and, sure enough, a few weeks later, the commercial ran." Cramer paused to chew on his cigar.

"Swartz was still leery, but the chance to score points with his bosses apparently won out over any suspicion in his mind, even though the sellout price was absurdly low—just a thousand each of the two times. Anyway, Swartz and Arnold dealt mostly by phone—with the anonymous Arnold always doing the calling, of course. But they did have two face-to-face encounters before the big blowup."

"When the money changed hands," Wolfe said.

"Right, old bills in a plain envelope and all that. And then, as you correctly pegged it, Swartz spotted Arnold's mug in the paper and saw an opportunity to make some really big money via the blackmail route."

"How big?" I asked.

Cramer turned to me. "Arnold says two hundred g's."

I whistled. "Swartz was a hungry rascal, wasn't he?"

"Yep, and as we all know, that appetite ended up costing him. After he saw the picture he called Arnold at the company office. He couldn't get through, but he left his name, which of course scared the bejesus out of Arnold. The rest pretty much tells itself—or I should say Wolfe told it the other night.

"Fearing the worst, Arnold called Swartz back and got the bad news. Frightened, he agreed to a meeting—it was in a coffee shop on Third Avenue—and that's when he learned what it would cost to keep Swartz quiet. Arnold agreed and said he needed a little time to get the dough together, but later he phoned Swartz and reneged, claiming two hundred big ones was too much, that he couldn't get the money without his father knowing about it. Swartz countered by saying he knew Annie Burkett at Mills/Lake/Ryman, and that he was going to call her immediately to set up a meeting to tell her the whole story. He was bluffing, of course, but he followed through on the call in case Arnold tried to check with her. He could always cancel their meeting if Arnold knuckled under, which of course he was counting on. In fact, I doubt if he planned to say anything to Miss Burkett as long as there was even the smallest chance to bleed Arnold."

I grinned. "Like you said before, Mr. Wolfe had it nailed."

"Uh-huh," Cramer nodded. "I'm not denying that. By now Arnold was more scared than ever, and he told Swartz he'd find a way to come up with the money. In his statement to us, he said he went to Swartz's apartment by prearrangement at five-thirty Tuesday to try to negotiate a payment plan, but Swartz insisted on getting the whole two hundred at once. They argued, and Arnold says Swartz threatened to go right to his old man to get payment. At that point, he says he panicked, and when Swartz turned his back, he picked up that award statue and hit him with it two or three times."

"Have the newspapers and the other media been informed of this yet?" Wolfe asked, pouring beer.

"No. God, he just got done making his statement a few minutes ago," Cramer said. "In fact, I should be back at headquarters, not here. And I suppose the minute I walk out that door, you'll be on the horn to Cohen. That gives the *Gazette* a nice head start, but I can't help that now, can I?"

"No sir, you can't. I appreciate the time you've taken to come here," Wolfe said as Cramer rose to leave, nodding curtly. His visit was a tribute to Wolfe, as close to an out-and-out compliment as the inspector is ever likely to dole out, and we both knew it. I followed him to the hall and went so far as to help him on with his coat. And he went so far as to say "thank you," showing just how mellow he was.

But that was okay, because for once, something that made Cramer happy made Wolfe happy, too.

TWENTY-ONE

The Arnold Foreman confession was big news, of course. The *Gazette* got its early jump on the competition, with that assist from Cramer, who also gave Wolfe a lot of credit in newspaper and TV interviews. Arnold's attorney made a stab at an insanity defense, but medical types testifying for the state shot holes in that strategy, and he was found guilty. The sentence was life, although as of this writing, appeals are being mounted, and the whole business will probably drag on for years.

The morning after the *Gazette* bannered the confession in three-inch capital letters, Rod Mills came to the house with a cashier's check for twenty-five thousand dollars. Wolfe was up with the orchids at the time, and Mills wasn't inclined to wait for his descent, which was forty minutes away. "Tell him thank you from me and my partners," he said, shaking my hand. "I hope he isn't angry that I withheld this until now." I answered that he wasn't. After all, why not be nice, especially since Wolfe wasn't there to contradict me?

Mills/Lake/Ryman doesn't have the Cherr-o-key account anymore. After Arnold's trial, Acker Foreman lost interest in the company and sold it to a British conglomerate that wanted to use another ad agency. According to the papers, Foreman took his multimillions from the sale and set up a trust that would make the Cherokees gladder than ever he was one of them, if only one-quarter's worth.

M/L/R seems to have survived the loss of the cherry drink reasonably well. I read this week in the *Times* that they just won the business of a feisty regional airline in the Southeast that proclaims itself "The Winning Wings." The reporter noted that this was the third new account the agency had gotten in the last six weeks, and Rod Mills was quoted in the same article, saying the three new pieces of business more than offset the loss of Cherr-o-key. And M/L/R also had held onto the Graffiti's account, although with a different commercial than the one Lake had shown me.

So Mills was hard at work doing his job—maybe too well. When Lily and I were out dancing the other night, she mentioned that Dawn Tillison wasn't going out with the adman anymore.

"Why not?" I asked. "Although I only saw them together once, there appeared to these old eyes to be a rather healthy mutual attraction."

"Dawn said he was a workaholic and she almost never got to see him. Escamillo, I'm glad you're not like that," Lily murmured, nuzzling me as we fox-trotted to "Me and My Shadow."

"Mills wouldn't be like that, either, if he had a Lily Rowan to look forward to being with after working hours," I said.

"Has anyone ever told you that you've got the knack for saying exactly the right thing at the right time?"

"Never," I said, giving her my most modest and winsome smile as we took another turn around the floor.

A NERO WOLFE MYSTERY

Here are special advance preview chapters from SILVER SPIRE, the new Nero Wolf novel by Robert Goldsborough, to be published in the Fall of 1992.

SILVER SPIRE
Robert Goldsborough

NERO WOLFE RETURNS
IN A BANTAM DOUBLE AUDIO
CASSETTE ABRIDGMENT
OF *SILVER SPIRE!*

CHAPTER 1

With two baritone belches of the horn, the *Samuel I. Newhouse* eased from its slip at South Ferry, and we were on the briny. It was the middle of the day, and only a couple of dozen people or so were scattered throughout the big boat, most of them either reading or dozing or trying to wriggle into comfortable positions on the molded, one-size-fits-all blue plastic seats.

The interior of the ferry had all the charm of a warehouse, and after five minutes of trying to get comfortable myself, I went out onto the small deck at the bow and let the May breeze blow across my face. The Statue of Liberty and Ellis Island, New York's newest tourist attraction, were off to the right—make that the starboard, mate—and the Verrazano-Narrows Bridge arched gracefully to port, while dead ahead through the haze of New York Harbor, the low green hills of Staten Island began to take form.

That morning as I sat in the kitchen of Nero Wolfe's brownstone on West Thirty-fifth Street devouring wheatcakes and the *Times*, I recalled the last time I had been on Staten Island, which most New Yorkers don't even think of as part of the city—when they think of it at all. That was almost ten years ago, when Wolfe took a case involving an arrogant old art collector on the island whose prized Cézanne had been filched from his house and replaced with a good but not great copy.

All arrows pointed to the collector's crotchety and somewhat larcenous maid, but it turned out the switch had been pulled by a guy posing as a gas company employee who said he'd been sent out to find a leak in the line. Anyway, thanks to Wolfe's brainpower and my leg power, the phony gas man, a onetime art history student with a police record as long as a pickpocket's fingers, got nailed, the Cézanne was recovered, and our bank balance received a healthy and much-needed transfusion.

This time, however, I was venturing forth to the Borough of Richmond on what both Wolfe and I considered far more momentous business. But then, I'm getting ahead of myself, so I'll start where they say you're supposed to start—at the beginning.

The beginning was a rainy May morning—a Thursday, if you're the type who insists on details. Wolfe was in the brownstone's rooftop greenhouse puttering with his orchids, as is his unvarying routine from nine to eleven every morning and four to six in the P.M. I sat at my desk in the office, entering orchid germination records into the personal computer, as is part of my own more or less unvarying routine.

The doorbell rang at ten-fourteen, and because the brownstone's Most Valuable Player, chef Fritz Brenner, was out buying provisions that later would be part of three-star meals, I did the honors, walking down the hall and peering through the one-way glass in the front door. The visitor on the stoop was high-shouldered and barrel-chested, and in his vested charcoal pinstripe, he looked like a banker faced with the prospect of having to give a loan, or maybe he was just suffering gas pains. But he didn't seem like the type to carry a concealed weapon, so I swung the door open.

"Good morning," I said with gusto. "We already have a set of Britannicas and currently subscribe to no fewer than eleven magazines—I can show you the list. Also, everyone who lives here is well insured, and we are not in the market for a vacuum cleaner, a set of genuine horsehair brushes, or a food processor. Now, what can I do for you, or you for me?"

I didn't even get a lip twitch for my efforts. "I am here to seek Nero Wolfe's counsel," the banker type intoned somberly. "May I assume that you are Archie Goodwin, his associate?"

"Assume to your heart's content," I said. "Before this conversation goes a single sentence further, however, I must warn you that Mr. Wolfe sees no one—repeat, no one—without an appointment. And because I am the keeper of the appointment book, I am keenly aware that you don't have one—an appointment, that is."

"Correct. I realize that I took a chance by coming here without calling first. Maybe that was an ill-conceived strategy, but I thought perhaps you, Mr. Goodwin, would be willing to hear my supplication and decide whether it merits Mr. Wolfe's consideration."

"That's a lot of syllables but I'm used to all that and more from my employer. Tell you what: If you promise not to toss too many more big words around, I'll hear your—what was it?—supplication. No guarantees, though."

"No guarantees," the banker type agreed, still pokerfaced.

"Another thing," I told him, planting myself in the doorway. "Is it fair to assume that your parents gave you a name?"

"What? Oh, yes, of *course*." He indulged in a chestheaving breath and made a pathetic stab at smiling. "Please excuse my manners. My name is Lloyd Morgan, and I work very closely with the Reverend Barnabas Bay."

"Bay as in that big church I've read about over on Staten Island, the one with the bells-and-whistles TV show?"

"The Tabernacle of the Silver Spire." Morgan pronounced the words proudly, as if they themselves were holy. "We feel our televised service is very tasteful, however."

"Well, anyway, that's the place," I said, ushering Morgan into the brownstone and down the hall to the office. I pointed him at the red leather chair in front of Wolfe's desk and slid in behind my own desk, swiveling to face him. "Mr. Wolfe is up playing with his orchids," I told our visitor, "and he won't be back down until eleven. But you have my undivided attention; what's the problem?"

Morgan considered the well-tended nails on his thick fingers, then took what I assume was a thoughtful breath before making eye contact. "First off, Barney—that's what Father Bay asks everybody on the staff to call him—knows I'm here, although he doesn't entirely approve. He thinks I'm a worrywart. That is the exact word he used: 'worrywart,' " Morgan said in an offended tone. "However, worrywart or not, I insisted that we needed outside help and told him about Nero Wolfe, whom he'd never heard of."

"The poor fellow must be living in a state of sensory deprivation," I deadpanned. "Everyone has heard of Nero Wolfe, probably even those Sherpa guides up on Mount Everest." Okay, so I was having a little fun at the poor guy's expense, mainly because I knew he wouldn't pick up on it. He didn't.

"Barney maintains an incredible schedule," Morgan went on without apology, defending his boss, which is always worth a few points in my book. "It seems like he's on the move every minute—a speech to the ministerial council in Newark, a benefit dinner for one of our shelters for the homeless in the Bronx, the mayor's prayer breakfast downtown. He probably doesn't always read the papers as thoroughly as he should."

"Maybe none of us does." I almost liked Morgan—but not quite. "Now that we've agreed on something, how do you see Nero Wolfe helping you and the good reverend?"

Morgan, who had primly declined my offer of coffee, did loosen to the extent of unbuttoning his suitcoat, which was progress. Then he cleared his throat several times, which was not. "Mr. Goodwin, may I assume that this conversation is confidential?"

"You may, unless a crime has been committed,

in which case, as a private investigator licensed by the sovereign State of New York, I am required to report said crime. No choice." Okay, so there have been a few times—make it quite a few—when I've done some fudging with that particular requirement.

Morgan tilted his head back, apparently trying to look superior. "No *actual* crime has been committed—yet. But we, at least some of us, are worried that one will be."

"So I gather. Go on."

More throat clearing. "You have, of course, never been to the Tabernacle."

"Correct." I nodded with a smile, mildly irked by the "of course" but amused by the disapproval in his voice.

"Well," he sniffed, "then you probably aren't aware that we get a total of some twelve thousand every Sunday attending our three morning services plus our evening service."

"Impressive. But I gather one of those twelve thousand is causing you and your leader grief."

"What makes you think that?"

I shrugged. "Give me a shred of credit. Look, for the last few minutes, we've been tiptoeing around each other like two cautious welterweights in round one. I could probably sit here for another hour or more trying to guess your problem, but I won't—I've got other things that I'm paid to do. Now I suggest you unload whatever it is you've got and let me see it before I get on with the rest of my life."

"All right, it's just that this is difficult to talk about," Morgan said stiffly. "For the last six Sundays, we've gotten very disturbing notes in the offering pouch—all directed at Barney."

"Pardon my ignorance, but what's an offering pouch?"

Another superiority sniff. "As I am sure you know, most churches send plates down the pews for the offering—the collection, if you will. But some, and we are among them, circulate cloth or leather pouches through the congregation—they have handles and they're about this deep," he said, holding one palm about a foot above the other. "For one thing, it's easier to be private about your offering if you're giving cash, and for another, our sanctuary is so big that if we passed conventional plates, they'd all overflow—even if we had twenty of them. The pouches hold a great deal more than a plate."

"Okay, so what do these 'disturbing notes' say?"

Morgan looked to be having more gas pains. "I've brought them." He sighed, reaching into his suitcoat and drawing out a packet of folded sheets that were paper-clipped together. He eyed me for several seconds, trying to decide whether I was trustworthy. Apparently I passed his trust test, if only barely. He handed over the small bundle, but turned loose of it like a widow giving her Social Security check to a bank teller.

"As I said, there are six notes," he told me, "arranged in the order in which they came."

I slipped the paper clip off, holding the sheets by the edges so as not to add my fingerprints to heaven knows how many others already there. The white sheets all were the same size, six by nine inches, probably from the same pad, and each had a message hand-printed in capitals in black ink from a felt-tipped pen. Here they are, in sequence:

REV BAY: MISFORTUNE PURSUES THE SINNER. (PROVERBS 13:21)

REV. BAY: TAKE YOUR EVIL DEEDS OUT OF MY SIGHT (ISAIAH 1:16)

REVEREND BAY: THE STING OF DEATH IS SIN (I CORINTHIANS 15:56)

REV. BAY: DEATH IS THE DESTINY OF EVERY MAN (ECCLESIASTES 7:2)

REVER. BAY: YOU DESERVE TO DIE. (I KINGS 2:26)

REV. BAY: THE TIME IS NEAR (REVELATIONS 1:13)

"Pretty ominous-sounding stuff," I said to Morgan. "Does your Mr. Bay get this sort of message often?"

"He does *not,*" he replied, squaring his shoulders and looking offended. "Oh, once in awhile, we find a note in the offering pouch expressing disapproval—usually mildly—about something in a sermon or in some other part of the service, which isn't unusual in a church our size. But this . . ."

"What does Bay think about the notes?"

"He professes indifference," Morgan said irritably. "Feels it's just the doings of some 'misguided soul,' to use his words."

"You don't agree, of course, or you wouldn't be here."

"Mr. Goodwin, these are the work of a psychopath, someone who I believe is truly dangerous."

"Maybe that's the case," I conceded, flipping open my notebook. "You say these have been coming for six weeks, which figures—there are six of them. Along about the third Sunday, didn't you, or someone else at the church, get suspicious and start watching more closely as the collection was taken?"

Morgan flushed. "We should have, of course. But we—Barney, me, the rest of the staff—all thought this was the work of a demented individual, maybe somebody who was just passing through New York and soon would be gone. We get a lot of one- or two-time visitors from out of town."

"Does Bay have any enemies? Or any secrets that would make him vulnerable to, say, blackmail?"

Lloyd Morgan shook his head almost violently. "No, sir, and I must tell you I resent that suggestion."

"Hold it right there. You walked in here—without an appointment, I hasten to point out—looking for help. Nobody twisted your arm to come. If you feel like doing any resenting, you can damn well do it outside, on your way back to Staten Island."

That deflated the boy's radials. "I'm sorry," he said, biting his lower lip and taking an economy-sized breath. "This has been stressful for all of us, and I guess it shows. As far as enemies, Barney doesn't have any that I'm aware of—or that he's aware of, to hear him talk. Oh, there are churches in the New York area that are jealous of his success, but it's inconceivable that one of their members would resort to this sort of despicable behavior."

"Uh-huh. How would you describe the makeup of your flock?"

Morgan leaned back and laced his hands behind his head, which suggested that I was about to get more answer than I'd requested.

"Mr. Goodwin, our membership, or 'flock,' as you so quaintly term it, is something over twelve thousand strong, and that's not to mention the tens of thousands in our 'electronic congregation,' who watch on TV from every single state, every Canadian province, and sixteen other countries, including Korea and the Philippines.

"Demographically, our members are a healthy mix. Of the twelve thousand plus, more than half are under thirty-five, and forty-four percent are single. And you'll probably be surprised to learn that almost four thousand of them live in Manhattan—many in the Village, East Village, and Soho. And several hundred ride over on the ferry. Would you have guessed that?"

"Never," I said solemnly.

That brought forth a thin smile, which Wolfe would have described as smug. "I thought not," he said in a satisfied tone that made me want to help him out the door.

"Have you begun any type of internal investigation, or tried to at least figure out where the note writer sits every week?"

"No. As I said before, we kept hoping it would . . . go away by itself."

"These things rarely do. What about the police?"

Morgan shuddered. "With due respect to the authorities, this is the last course we want to pursue—at least at this point. As you of course know, the past few years have been difficult ones for high-profile ministries, particularly ones with a television arm. Now, I don't for one instant mean to compare us with some of the evangelists you've heard all too much about in the media. But the fact is, because of them and the awful image they have, we are very skittish about any kind of publicity that could be construed as sensational. And we are concerned that if we called in the police, word would inevitably get to the press. Now do you see why I asked earlier if our talk was confidential?"

"I do. But if the situation worries you as much as you indicate, doesn't it really warrant bringing in the police?'

"Perhaps eventually." Morgan nodded. "But we—Barney, me, the other church leaders—thought that we'd try an alternative first, and that alternative is Nero Wolfe."

"All right. But there are a couple things you should know from the start. First, Mr. Wolfe doesn't come cheap, and—"

"We are prepared to meet all but the most exorbitant demands," Morgan announced pompously.

"And you may well find Mr. Wolfe's demands exorbitant. But second, and this you can't do a damn thing about, he also is far from the world's biggest fan of organized religion—regardless of who's doing the organizing. Now that I've said that, don't ever make the mistake of trying to duel with him over biblical quotes; he knows that book better than I know the batting averages of the last Mets championship team. And believe me, I can give you those figures right down to earned-run averages."

Morgan passed a handkerchief across his dewy forehead and sighed. "So are you suggesting that we look elsewhere for aid?"

"Not necessarily. But I do feel you should know exactly how the cards lie, and frankly, I'm not sure you have openers. However, Mr. Wolfe will be in the office in twelve minutes, and I'll discuss the matter with him then. How can I reach you?"

Morgan reached into the breast pocket of his suitcoat and after some fumbling, he produced a calling card, a tasteful buff-colored number with his name in the center, the church's in the lower left corner, and the phone number lower right.

"Just for the record," I said, "what's your role at the Tabernacle?"

"Business manager." He sniffed. "A 'Mr. Inside,' if you will, while Barney of course is "Mr. Outside.' He's our star, as it should be. He preaches almost every Sunday, and he's the one the TV audience sees. I'm just a paperpusher back in the office." He smiled modestly—or maybe he wanted it to appear modest.

"One more thing," I told him. "I'd like to keep these notes, just long enough to show them to Mr. Wolfe. They may help pique his interest. I promise I'll return them to you intact—whether or not Mr. Wolfe takes the case."

Morgan looked at the notes doubtfully and then shrugged. "I didn't really intend to leave them. Well . . . all right, if you promise that I'll get them back."

"I promise. Do you want a receipt?'

"No, no, your word is more than good enough, Mr. Goodwin," he said, not sounding as if he meant it.

"Okay, then this is all I need for now," I told him as I stood up.

He also got to his feet, looking uncertain. "When will I hear from you?"

"Today. Will you be in your office?"

He said he would and I hustled him out as

politely as possible, all the while reassuring him I would call him before day's end. I didn't like the odds of Wolfe's accepting Morgan and Bay as clients, but I knew the bank balance was in need of nourishment, so I had at least some leverage with Wolfe.

CHAPTER 2

Back at my desk after letting Morgan out, I still had ten minutes before Wolfe's arrival from his morning séance with the orchids. I put the time to use by calling Lon Cohen at the *New York Gazette*.

Lon has no title at the paper that I've ever heard of or seen in print, and his name is not on the paper's masthead. But he occupies an office next door to the publisher's on the twentieth floor, and he seems to know more about what goes on in New York, both above board and below, than the City Council and the Police Department combined. He has provided useful information to us on at least a gross of occasions, and we've reciprocated by giving the *Gazette* at least as many scoops. And, not incidentally, he also plays a mean hand of stud poker, as I rediscover to my sorrow almost every Thursday night at Saul Panzer's apartment, where several of us have gathered with the pasteboards for years.

"Morning," I said after he'd answered his phone with the usual bark of his name. "Got a minute for a friend?"

"I haven't got a minute for my mother, let

alone the mother of my children. What makes you special?"

"Ah, a bit on the testy side today, are we? You shouldn't be terse with someone who so thoughtfully lined your pockets with lettuce at the gaming table a week ago this very day."

"I *did* have a pretty fair night, didn't I?" Lon responded, sounding almost mellow. "All right, what do you need to know? And what's in it for me?"

"Now there's a cynical attitude," I said. "See if I raise tonight when you've got a pair showing."

"Archie, I'd just love to go on bantering all morning, but at the risk of sounding like somebody from *The Front Page*, we've got a paper to put out."

"And a fine paper it is, me lad. Okay, what can you tell me in a few well-chosen sentences about the Reverend Barnabas Bay and his big church over on Staten Island?"

"Bay? He's got a reputation for being smart, damned smart. Comes originally from someplace down south, maybe Georgia. He's built a big following here in just a few years, and a huge building. Its name is a little too show bizzy for me—the Tabernacle of the Silver Spire. It's got that name because the church, which is nondenominational, is topped by a metal spire, stainless steel or aluminum, I suppose, that dwarfs everything else around it. Controversial when it was built. But, at least according to our religion writer, Bay's several cuts above the televangelists who've supplied us with so many juicy headlines in the none-too-distant past. By all accounts, he's honest, earnest, and one hell of a spellbinder in the pulpit."

"Any hint of scandal?"

"Not that's come my way. No personal stuff I've ever heard about. He's got a wife who's a knockout, and I think four kids. About two years back, a handful of churches on the island and over in Jersey complained that they'd lost parishioners to him, but that happens all the time. Might just be that he's giving 'em something they weren't getting from their local pastors."

"The guy sounds too good to be true."

"That's exactly what I told Walston—he's our religion writer—after reading the Sunday piece he did on Bay a while back. But Walston said that's the real Bay. And the padre puts his money—or the church's money—where his mouth is. The Silver Spire has set up several shelters for battered women and the homeless in Manhattan, and the church supplies all the money and staffing to support them, the works. Okay, I've given you more than a few sentences; what can you give me, as in, one: why is Wolfe interested in Bay? And, two: does the good reverend have feet of clay after all?"

"I don't have answers, because I don't know myself—honest. But you can rest assured that if anything happens, you'll be hearing from us."

"Yeah, and the check's in the mail, right?" Lon growled, signing off with a mumble that sounded vaguely like "good-bye." Cradling the receiver, I just got the day's mail opened and stacked on Wolfe's blotter before the groaning of the elevator heralded his arrival from on high.

"Good morning, Archie, did you sleep well?" he asked as he detoured around the desk and settled into the chair constructed specifically to support his seventh of a ton. It's a question he's asked on thousands of mornings.

"Like a baby," I answered, as I have on thousands of mornings.

So much for one of our daily rituals. He spun through the mail quickly, given that it held nothing of interest, then pushed the buzzer on the underside of his desk. It squawks in the kitchen, signaling Fritz to bring beer—specifically, two bottles of Remmers. He then picked up his current book, *Mars Beckons,* by John Noble Wilford, which he was intending to read until lunch.

"Before you get smitten with the idea of hitching a ride on the next Mars-bound rocket, we had a visitor this morning," I told him.

He set the book down deliberately and looked peevish, his normal expression when his routine is messed with. I got an "All right, what is it?" glare, although his lips didn't move.

"A gentleman stopped by," I began as Fritz entered silently, bearing a tray with two bottles of beer and a pilsner glass. "This gentleman's boss is getting threatening notes, and he wants to hire you to find out who's writing them."

The peevish expression remained as Wolfe poured beer and watched the foam settle. "Continue," he said coldly.

"You know as well as I do what the current state of our finances is," I responded.

Wolfe drew in air and let it out slowly, keeping his narrowed eyes on me. "Archie, you are maundering," he snorted. "I am painfully aware that I will get no peace until you have unburdened yourself. Let's get on with it."

This was going to be tricky. "You remember

how you once said that a client's line of work is far less important than the problem he presents to us?"

"I expressed that thought in relation to a specific and unusual situation, as you well remember."

"Through the years, we've had a lot of unusual situations, and for my money, we have another one." I looked at Wolfe and got no encouragement, but I've never been one to let that stop me. "The man on the receiving end of the threatening notes is well-known," I went on. "Maybe you've heard of him; his name is Barnabas Bay."

"Pah. A clerical mountebank."

"Pah yourself. I know you have a lot of respect for the knowledge and opinions of our friend Mr. Cohen. He tells me that Bay is far from a mountebank, and that—"

"You don't even know the definition of the word," Wolfe challenged.

"Wrong. I looked it up after it had been used to describe *you* by someone in this very room a few years back. And at that, she was the second person to call you a mountebank. One more and I'm going to start believing it. Anyway, Lon describes Bay as smart, honest, earnest, and a top-drawer preacher to boot. To say nothing of the good works his church does, among them shelters here in Manhattan for battered women and the homeless."

"Commendable," Wolfe answered without conviction. "Suggest that he talk to the police about the notes."

"I did, but, at least according to his sidekick, Lloyd Morgan—he's the man who stopped by—

Bay is trying to avoid the kind of publicity that might result from an investigation."

"Given his line of work, his reaction would seem a prudent one," Wolfe said.

"That sounds suspiciously like a cheap shot," I told him. "How about asking me for a verbatim report of my chat with Mr. Morgan?"

Wolfe sighed and closed his eyes, probably hoping I would disappear. "It appears that I'll get one whether I want it or not. Go ahead."

In the past, I've recounted conversations of hours in length to Wolfe without omitting a single word, so this shorty was a snap. I ended by placing the notes in front of him. "Here, you may find these interesting," I said.

Wolfe made a face but studied the sheets in silence for ninety seconds, careful not to touch them with his fingertips. "Anyone with a concordance could have done this all in ten minutes, fifteen at most," he said, waving a hand.

"Okay, I'm willing to concede that there's a gap in my knowledge: what's a concordance?'

"A refreshing admission. It is a biblical subject index. Many Bibles have them in the back. Return these to Mr. Morgan," he said curtly, pushing the notes in my direction.

"What should I tell him?"

"To go to the police, of course," he snapped, picking up his book. If I've learned anything at all about the foibles of genius in the years of living in the same household with one, it's knowing when to keep after him and when to back off. This was one of those times to back off—if only for a while. I left Wolfe to his beer and book and busied myself with the orchid germination records, which kept me occupied until lunchtime.

Among the unwritten rules in the brownstone is that business—and that includes prospective business—is not to be discussed during meals. So as we feasted on Maryland crabcakes and Fritz's Caesar salad with garlic croutons, Wolfe held forth on the advisability of the United States reorganizing into about a dozen states— certainly no more than fifteen. I mostly listened, chewed, and nodded, although I did ask who the rest of the country would make jokes about if there wasn't a California to kick around anymore.

As usual, we returned to the office after lunch for coffee, but I still wasn't ready to renew the Bay campaign. Wolfe read until it was time to visit his orchids at four, while I balanced the checkbook, paid the bills, and reread the *Gazette*'s account of the zany Mets game against Cincinnati at Shea, in which our boys scored six runs in the second inning on only one hit, a bunt single. Shows you what can happen when the opponents make three errors, hit a batter, give you three walks, and throw a wild pitch.

After Wolfe went upstairs, I called Morgan, who picked up on the first ring. "You talked to him?" he blurted before could spit out anything other than my name.

"Yes, but I have nothing definite to report. We're going to discuss your problem again later."

"Oh dear, that doesn't sound terribly encouraging, does it?"

"Now, I didn't say that. I promised to report today, though, and I wanted to make sure I caught you before you went home. I'll phone you again in the morning."

Morgan didn't sound tickled with the news, but that was his problem; I had my own—getting Wolfe to take a church as a client. I tried him again when he came down from the plant rooms at six, and I'll spare you the grim details, other than to say that he got so angry with my badgering, as he calls it, that he stalked out of the office, retreating to his bedroom until dinnertime. And following dinner, as we got settled in the office with coffee, I tried once more, pointing out to Wolfe that he didn't have to go near the Silver Spire church himself.

"As usual, I'll do all the on-site work," I told him, "and for that matter, you don't have to be exposed to Bay or any of his religious types until the very end, when you've figured the thing out."

His answer was a glower and two sentences: "Archie, let me save your larynx further exercise on this subject. Under no circumstances will I accept a commission from Mr. Bay or his organization."

"Un-huh. The bank balance be hanged, eh? What do you suggest I say to Morgan?"

Wolfe turned a hand over. "Tell him whatever you like. This is not the first time we have rejected an entreaty, nor is it likely to be the last."

"Keep your pronouns in the first person where they belong," I shot back. "*I* didn't reject anything."

Wolfe glowered again and retreated behind his book, which gave me some satisfaction, but not much. I contemplated quitting, something I've done for varying periods at least a dozen times over the years, but vetoed the idea because my vacation was coming up in less than a month, and Lily

Rowan and I had all our reservations for two weeks in England and Scotland. True, I had a respectable amount squirreled away in savings and a few investments, but I was damned if I was going to let Wolfe off the hook for my well-earned furlough—with pay.

Fortunately, I had a good reason to leave the brownstone that night, thereby possibly saving Wolfe from being brained with a blunt object and me from being booked on a murder charge. It was Thursday, meaning I had the above-mentioned engagement with cards and chips—both the poker and potato variety—at Saul's place over on Thirty-eighth just east of Lexington. And this time, I was the big winner, while Lon—who never once mentioned Barnabas Bay—went home with empty pockets.

The next morning, while Wolfe was up with the orchids, I called Lloyd Morgan from my desk in the office. "Sorry to be the bearer of bad news," I told him, "but Mr. Wolfe does not feel he can accept your problem."

I could hear an intake of air. "I was afraid of that," he said. "I gather that decision is irreversible?"

"I'm afraid so."

Another deep breath. "Is there . . . anyone else you could recommend? Perhaps another investigator?"

For those of you who are new to these precincts, when the need arises, as it frequently does, Wolfe employs two freelances—Saul Panzer and Fred Durkin. Saul doesn't look like much: barely five-seven, skinny, stoop-shouldered, usually in need of a shave, and with a face that's two-thirds nose. But he's got a sharper pair of eyes than

Willie Mays in his prime, and when assigned to follow someone, he sticks to him—or her—like epoxy. He's also in constant demand, and has more work than he can handle, although he'll almost always drop whatever he's doing for Wolfe.

Fred Durkin is another story. He's big—make that thick—somewhat on the slow side, and a long way from brilliant. He doesn't give up anything in the bravery department, though, with loyalty and honesty two more of his strong suits. And while he's no Saul, he's tenacious and damn good as a tail. Through the years, Wolfe has used him almost as much as Saul, but of late, business has been slow, which Fred has complained to me about more than once. Maybe this was one part of the reason I was leaning Fred's way when Morgan posed his question. The other part was that the job didn't seem all that complicated on the surface.

Maybe you'd have done it differently. If so, I wish you'd been around that Friday morning to stop me before I gave Fred's telephone number to Lloyd Morgan. Then you wouldn't be reading this.

CHAPTER 3

For the next eleven days, I barely gave a thought to the Tabernacle of the Silver Spire or to Lloyd Morgan or Fred Durkin. Part of the reason was that I had nudged Wolfe into accepting an honest-to-goodness case—although not a very exciting one—involving a small supermarket chain whose largest store, up in Westchester County, was coming up short on its receipts almost every day. The culprit, as Wolfe suspected early on based on my nosing around the store for two days, was a debt-laden assistant manager who had two accomplices—a pair of rosy-cheeked young checkout girls, both teenagers, with the most innocent faces this side of a convent. Our fee wasn't breathtaking, but given that the whole business took less than a week, we had no reason to complain.

Another distraction—a pleasant one—was that La Rowan got more fired up by the day about our trip to Merrie Olde, and that enthusiasm started to rub off on yours truly, to the point that I was digesting guidebooks about places like the Lake Country and the Cotswolds and Loch Lomond. Oh, did hear from Fred once, the very day I'd recommended him to Morgan. He called to find out what I knew about the church, as well as asking why Wolfe had shied away from accepting the case.

"Mr. Wolfe avoids most things having to do with formal religion," I told him. I also gave him my impressions of Morgan, along with Lon's comments about Bay as a preacher and spiritual leader. I signed off by saying "Good luck, and give a holler if you need anything," and I sent the threatening notes back to Morgan in a sealed envelope—at my expense—via Herb Aronson, for my money the most dependable cabbie in New York.

The holler, when I got it, came from another quarter. It was a Tuesday morning about nine, and I was in the office typing up letters Wolfe had dictated the day before when the phone rang.

"Okay, Archie, better catch me up, and fast!" It was Lon Cohen, and the exclamation mark I put on the end of his sentence doesn't do justice to the urgency in his voice.

"Catch you up on what?"

"You know damn well what," he blurted. "The Silver Spire business, and Durkin."

"What about Durkin?" Now I was almost shouting myself, and my throat suddenly got as dry as Death Valley.

"As if you didn't know. He's been tossed in the slammer—for murder."

"Wha-a-a-t? How did—"

"Dammit, Archie, stop jerking me around. We're coming up on the deadline for an edition, and I've got to have something fast. The boss knows Durkin's practically an employee of Wolfe's, and he's all over me to come up with an exclusive on this."

My brain was racing to keep pace with my mouth. "Bay's dead?"

"Not *Bay,*" Lon snapped irritably. "An assistant of his. Are you going to help me, or not?"

"Time out," I said. "First, Mr. Wolfe—through me— was approached by one of the Silver Spire staff because of a problem they were having; that's when I called you to find out about Bay. But Mr. Wolfe wasn't excited at the idea of having a church on his client list, so we recommended Fred."

Lon snorted. "I think I've been around you long enough to know you wouldn't throw Durkin to the dogs just to save your hide and Wolfe's. So you're giving it to me straight?"

"As straight as William Tell's arrow. Who got killed, and when?"

"Guy named Royal Meade, the senior associate pastor, and Bay's number two person on the staff. Durkin shot him sometime last night in one of the church offices."

"Bull. Did Fred confess?"

"All right, *allegedly* shot him. Anyway, he's downtown in the lockup. I'm surprised you hadn't heard about it. Now, just what kind of problem was the church having?"

"That's going to have to wait until I've spoken to my employer."

"Come on, Archie. We need—"

"Look, I've got to talk to Wolfe, and then I'll get back to you—I promise. Has a bond been set?"

"Oh, sure, you want information, but you're not willing to cough any up yourself," he snapped. "As far as bond, I don't know."

I vowed to Lon that he'd hear from me before the morning was over and I signed off, taking the stairs two at a time to the plant rooms. In the cool room, which is the first one you enter, I tried not to be dazzled by the reds and whites and yellows of the odontoglossums, but as often as I've been up on the roof, I never get used to the breathtaking sight of those and the other showoffs that make up the ten thousand orchids Wolfe refers to as his "concubines." I passed on through the moderate and tropical rooms, steeling myself against the charms of the cattleyas and miltonias.

Wolfe, wearing a yellow smock, was in the potting room, planted on his stool at the bench glumly considering a raceme of *Oncidium altissimum,* while Theodore Horstmann, Wolfe's full-time orchid nurse, was at the sink washing out pots.

Wolfe's expression didn't improve when he spotted me in the doorway. "Yes?" he grunted.

"We've got a problem, or you know damn well I wouldn't be up here," I said as old Horstmann threw a glare my way. He glares at me even when I'm not trespassing in his sanctuary, though. He doesn't like me, but that's okay, because the feeling is mutual and has been for years. I returned the glare, which sent him back to washing his pots.

"Durkin's in jail on a murder charge," I told Wolfe. "You recall I told you he took the Silver Spire job that you nixed. Well, some guy named Meade on the church staff got himself shot dead last night, and Lon called to tell me they've charged Fred."

"Preposterous."

"Agreed. What do we do?"

He drew in air and looked down at the raceme in his hand before gently placing it on the bench. "Confound it, get Mr. Parker—now."

Wolfe yields to no one in his distaste for the legal profession. However, he makes an exception for Nathaniel Parker, who has been his attorney for years and is one of the few men of any occupation he will shake hands with and invite to dinner. I went to the extension on the potting room wall and punched out Parker's number from memory. "Nero Wolfe calling," I told his secretary, who put me through, and I handed the receiver to Wolfe.

"Mr. Parker, Nero Wolfe. Yes, I am well, thank you. One of my associates, Fred Durkin, who you have met, has been charged with murder. . . . No, the circumstances are unclear. I'm putting Archie on to give you those few particulars he knows. . . . Yes, I am prepared to post bond." He handed the instrument to me, and I unloaded what Lon had given me. Parker took it in, said we'd be hearing from him shortly, and hung up. I cradled the phone, turning to Wolfe, who had resumed his seat at the bench.

"Okay, you're rid of me for now—except that I promised Lon I'd give him something for the next edition. We owe him that much for his call. I'd like to at least tell him about the notes."

His chin dipped almost imperceptibly, which for him constitutes a nod. He was so peeved at the interruption in his precious routine that he would have agreed to almost anything to get rid of me. As I walked out, I looked over my shoulder; Wolfe already had turned his attention back to the ailing

Oncidium, but Horstmann was at the sink eyeing me, probably afraid I'd walk off with something, like maybe an empty pot. I gave him a smile and a wink.